MW01699780

Mags

KATHLEEN O'CONNOR

DEDICATION

'I am the Way, the Truth, and the Life.'(Jn.14:6)

'Without the Way there is no going,
Without the Truth there is no knowing,
Without the Life there is no living.'
(Thomas á Kempis)

For their loving ministry in the service of the Lord,
I dedicate this book to "Immanuel Healing Ministry Group"
Castledermot, Co. Kildare.

May the Lord bless you and be with you always.

MAGS-
THE THIRD PART IN A HUGELY SUCCESSFUL
TRILOGY

INTRODUCTION

Peggy O'Flaherty climbed out of a window and into our hearts 3 years ago in Kathleen O'Connor's 'A Question For Heaven,' the first installment in her phenomenally successful trilogy. But Peggy was only the first in a line of proud, spirited Irish women Kathleen O'Connor was to bring vibrantly to life. Peggy's daughter Alana inherited all her mother's fierce, self-sacrificing willpower, single-mindedly following her vocation to the convent. But her sister Deirdre inherited instead an abundance of her mother's youthful romantic passion. A passion which sought fulfillment in excesses of alcohol, wealth, and most disastrously of all, men. A passion which eventually would carry her to the point of crisis, and carry her sister out of the convent to rescue her.

'A Question For Heaven' and 'Stepping Stones', the lively second installment, trace the aftermath of this crisis in both women's lives, along the way giving us a remarkable family's story of wealth, tragedy and love. With 'Mags', the trilogy's thrilling conclusion, Kathleen O'Connor gives us Peggy's grandchild, Mags O'Dowd - a heroine with all of Alana's indomitable will, coupled with all of Deirdre's lust for life. The result is an unquenchable ambition to have it all, no matter what the cost. The action moves us to the glitzy shores of America, and the high life of cocaine, parties and movie stardom. But like the women before her, no matter what the world has to offer her, what Mags must finally come to terms with is her own heart.

First published in Great Britain and Ireland 1991 by
Emperor Publishing an imprint of Glencree Publications
Limited.
27/29 Washington Street, Cork, Republic of Ireland.
© Kathleen O'Connor 1991
ISBN 0-9515271-9-3
Printed in Great Britain by
Cox & Wyman Ltd, Reading.

All rights reserved. No part of this publication may be reproduced or transmitted in any form or by any means, electronic or mechanical, including photography, recording, or any information storage or retrieval system, without permission in writing from the publisher. This book is sold subject to the condition that it shall not, by way of trade or otherwise, be lent, re-sold, hired out or otherwise circulated without the publisher's prior consent in any form of binding or cover other than that in which it is published and without a similar condition including this condition being imposed on the subsequent publisher.

PROLOGUE

He was the most familiar visitor to Sacramento General Hospital, this lovely old Franciscan priest, with the long grey beard and the kindliest of faces. Day after day he walked down the hospital corridors in his long, brown habit and bare, sandalled feet. He sought out the sick, the depressed, the old, the lonely, the homeless, the rejected. They were his children, precious to him, his life's work, and it was for them he constantly prayed. He didn't bring flowers, candy, fruit or any sort of material gift. As he often said himself, "I am as poor as a church mouse." What he did bring to his friends were words of hope, comfort, and love. And, irrespective of class or creed, they all loved Dom, as he was affectionately known.

As he sat on the threadbare armchair in his cell, reading his breviary one hot, humid night in late June, the phone hanging on the wall beside him rang. He got up slowly and answered it.

"Dom speaking."

"Hello, Father Dominic," came the bright, cheery voice.

Dom was slightly nonplussed.

"Can I help you?"

"It's me. You remember me, don't you?"

He was silent for a second, jogging his memory. The line was bad and he did not really recognise the voice. Thankfully, she helped him along.

"We met just recently at the hospital. You gave my husband the last rites and you heard my confession."

He still couldn't remember, not even a glimmer of recollection registered in his mind. There had been so many.

"You could never forget me, surely," she continued. "I'm the bad one, the one who broke all the commandments. Remember?"

A loving, gentle smile flickered across his worn, wrinkled face. It had been during his trip to Ireland just a few weeks ago. Oh what a happy trip that had been! He only wished he could have had more time with his family. He had met this pregnant woman one night when visiting the hospital in Cork. She truly had led a troubled, sinful past, but she'd unburdened herself to him. Her husband had been in a bad accident, Dom recalled. Had he passed on? Anyway, the woman, Margaret Anne, had actually grown up outside San Diego and had asked him to baptise her baby if she could at all make it to Sacramento. She must be in town, then.

"Oh yes, of course I remember. In Ireland. Margaret Anne, how could I ever forget that pretty face and those big, blue eyes? How are you? And did your husband ..."

"He's recovered completely."

"Oh, thank the Lord."

"We're both fine, and guess what? We have a beautiful baby daughter just two weeks old."

"Congratulations, I'm so very happy for you both. God love and bless you."

"And do you remember what we spoke about at the hospital? We were wondering if you would baptise her? Oh please say yes, it would mean such a lot to us."

"I am honoured and privileged to be asked, just tell me where and when. If you like I can arrange for it at --"

"No, I prefer to have it at the Sacred Heart Church, next Friday week."

The priest puckered his eyebrows. He had never heard of such a place in Sacramento. Perhaps it was in her home parish in San Diego.

"How far away is that? I must confess I do not know it."

"About three thousand miles away, on the southwest coast of Ireland."

He was totally taken aback.

"You said you were coming here with the baby. My darling child, I couldn't afford to take a bus to the next block. I've only just spent what my family had to spare during the trip I met you on."

"Don't you worry, I came up with a better plan. It's all arranged. Gordon and I will take care of everything. Your ticket will be at Los Angeles Airport and we'll meet you at Shannon. We have a nice, quiet hotel and you will stay there as our guests for as long as you like. Though I'm sure you'll be anxious to see your family as well. So, what do you say, Dom?"

Dom's heart melted and he was on the verge of tears. "What a lovely thought. Oh, to see Ireland again and spend more time with my dear family. It would be beyond my wildest dreams."

"So you'll come?"

"I would love with all my heart to baptise your child, Margaret Anne, my dear, but the decision is not mine. I will have to get permission from my superiors."

"They'll never refuse you, they wouldn't be so hard-hearted. What do you think, will they allow it?"

"If the good Lord wills it, I'll be there."

PART ONE -- AMERICA

CHAPTER 1

As she lay in the giant four-poster bed in the large, ultra-modern bedroom on Pacific Boulevard, San Diego, Margaret Anne tried to reconstruct the events of the last few months. She couldn't be absolutely sure whether she had done the things at all or simply imagined the whole series.

It had all begun with the baby. Because of the baby she had lost her job at Star Enterprises. Because of the baby she had to return with her parents to Ireland, had to be checked into St Helen's, had to wait for it to be born.

"Just take it away the minute it's born and do whatever you want with it," she'd told her mother.

She wanted no part of that baby. She'd refused to even look at it. What she wanted was money -- money, fame, and a good time. No way was she cut out to be a mother. She'd had no idea who the father was, nor did she care. She just wanted to be rid of the problem as soon as possible and then get back to her fast-paced life. God, how she was dying for a fix.

She remembered the nurse who'd come in to show her her baby and how she'd buried her head in her pillow.

"Are you quite sure of what you're doing?" the nurse had asked her. "He's a perfect little darling. If you would only look at him, you would love him immediately."

"Take him away," she'd insisted adamantly.

She remembered sitting alone in that room afterwards. She'd been uncomfortably aware of her swollen breasts and still-swollen stomach. What would her old boss, Gordon Edwards, who'd always said that she was the prettiest girl at Star Enterprises, think of her now?

She'd taken the little mirror from her cosmetic bag. No harm to her face anyway. Her skin was as perfect and unblemished as ever. She was determined, however, to rid herself of those unsightly lumps and bumps. That was her main objective.

She was plucking her eyebrows when Gráinne, her mother, arrived.

"You're looking very well today. Nobody would ever think that only a short while ago you gave birth to a bouncing baby boy."

Margaret Anne had completely ignored her mother's remark, but Gráinne continued undaunted.

"He's adorable, a perfect little beauty. He has a head of jet-black hair, the biggest eyes I have ever seen, and his little white baby grow accentuates his lovely dark skin."

Margaret Anne dropped the tweezers. Dark skin? As soon as Gráinne said those two words, she knew instantly who the father was.

The baby had gone to her cousin Gavin and his wife Bríd. The officials had told her that legally she had six months to reconsider, but Margaret Anne assured them that they had nothing to fear on that score. She'd returned to California as soon as she was able.

Gavin had been confined to a wheelchair for years after a bad fall he'd had trying to escape a fire. The doctors had told him that he would never be able to father a child. So it was with understandable joy that he and Bríd took in Margaret Anne's child. Nor for a second did they care that the baby was coloured. They called him Georgie, after Gavin's father. Georgie gave Gavin a new lease on life. Within weeks they realised a pram was unnecessary. Gavin wheeled Georgie around with him everywhere.

Lying in the huge bed, Margaret Anne shook aside the memory of Gavin. She recalled instead how she'd returned home to her apartment in San Diego after the ordeal was over, feeling as if a huge weight had been released. She was sure her life was about to take off. She remembered herself dancing around her apartment, kicking aside empty beer bottles and cans, tripping gaily over soiled clothes, empty Chinese food cartons, and cigarette packs. The dirty dishes could almost walk out the kitchen door to meet her, but what the hell? She sang and danced more wildly than ever, her spinning movements launching her into the bathroom. She caught sight of herself in the mirror and stopped.

"Hey, you're very pale, aren't you, Margaret Anne?" she said aloud to herself. "And look at those swollen, bloodshot eyes, and that tossed blonde hair."

She threw off the dirty, white sweat shirt and grubby blue jeans, went to the closet in her bedroom, and took out the pink dress that Gordon had given her for her birthday. Gordon was gone now, as were all her other boyfriends, but she didn't care. With the coke in her, nothing seemed to matter.

No, nothing, she decided, taking her last sniff. It didn't seem to matter anymore that every cent she had earned had been pumped into her nostrils, that her rent was three months in arrears, that all her credit cards had been confiscated, and that her pride and joy, the little, yellow Triumph Spitfire, had been repossessed three days ago.

She'd needed cash that day, so a trip to the parents' house was on the cards. She put drops into her eyes, so as not to advertise the fact that she was stoned. She threw on her navy anorak and left the apartment. Her friend Nicky gave her a lift out to Chula Vista.

There'd been nobody home at her parents' house when she arrived.

"This is my lucky day," she said, running upstairs to Eoin and Gráinne's bedroom.

The key to her father's bureau hung on a little nail at the back of the huge picture of Shandon that hung above the bed. She ran down to the study, opened the drawer where he kept his cash, and rummaged around. Not even a dollar.

She'd then rooted through presses in the kitchen. Her mother had a habit of keeping money in cups and teapots. Again she dew a blank. She was frantic now as she searched all through the house for any cash at all. She needed it so badly. Then her eyes fell on the framed photograph standing on the television set. A little, dark-skinned, beautiful baby. Instantly she knew it was her son.

Hell, she thought, he's an exact miniature of his father. Suddenly memories were triggered of her night in Thaida Khan's penthouse on Pacific Boulevard. She had to be stoned out of her mind to go to bed with him. But the large cheque he gave her kept her going in her expensive habits for two weeks.

It was then, staring at that picture in her parent's house, that she'd made up her mind. She would use her head, not her heart. She reached out and snatched the photograph. This would be her passport to the good life, plenty of cash, luxurious living quarters, and servants to wait on her hand and foot. Thaida wouldn't bother her much. Didn't he spend most of his time travelling around his chain of high class restaurants all over the west coast? She could cope with him for the weekends as long as she had plenty of drugs taken. She rooted in her handbag, found his card, and dialled his number.

"The Khan residence," the voice at the other end had answered.

"I'd like to speak to Thaida, please."

"Who may I say is calling?"

"Margaret Anne. He'll know who I am."

Her heart beat for seconds until she heard his thickly-accented voice.

"How are you, my sweet one?"

"Lonely for you," she lied.

"My poor pretty little Margaret Anne. But where are you?"

She gave him the address and he promised he would be on the doorstep within the hour. Poor, old fool, Margaret Anne thought, as she fixed her make-up in the bathroom mirror.

"We're in business, you and I," she said to her reflection.

She'd been peering through the window when the big, silver Rolls Royce drove smoothly up the avenue. The uniformed black chauffeur came out and rang the door bell.

"You miss Margaret Anne?"

"That's me."

Tyrone had then led her to the car and opened the rear door for her. Gathering her breath, she'd stepped inside. There was Thaida, sitting there and grinning like a Cheshire cat as the car pulled away. He was as she remembered him -- small, chubby, and, Margaret Anne guessed, about fifty years of age. His hair was jet- black and very greasy. He wore a neatly-trimmed, black moustache which he now stroked. He wore a white blazer with some sort of wine-coloured crest on it, wine trousers, and a shirt of the same colour. Each finger on each of his hands was adorned with a huge diamond ring, and he smoked a fat cigar. She settled in beside him and he held her hand.

"What is on your mind, my pretty one?" he'd asked. "You can tell Thaida. He can take care of everything."

"Let's go for a drive," she smiled. "We can talk later."

"Where would you like to go, my darling?"

"I need some clothes. I want to look good for you. Will you take me to Plaza Bonita, please?" she asked, kissing him.

It was an effort to fall into his waiting arms. But she knew this old sugar daddy would pay dearly for her love and affection.

She was very glad when Tyrone reached the car park of the Plaza and stopped the car. She extricated herself from his clutches and ran a brush through her hair. Thaida withdrew his wallet.

"How much will these clothes be?" he asked.

"Five hundred should be enough," she said, trying to sound calm. She needed a fix very badly now.

He counted out the bills slowly and asked, "Would you like me to come in with you? I have excellent taste in lady's clothes."

"No, no, I want to surprise you."

She'd then rushed inside, met her contact at the usual place in the restaurant upstairs and scored her supply of cocaine. She'd gone to the rest room immediately and taken her first sniff. Then she'd rushed downstairs and bought the cheapest black nightie she could find. He won't have a clue of the price, she'd reasoned to herself.

Later that night had come the moment she'd been fortifying herself for. Thaida had lifted her in his chubby arms and lain her on the white, satin sheets of the giant bed -- the very bed where fifteen months before their son had been conceived.

Margaret Anne had looked at Thaida with a mixture of anticipation and anxiety. He looked almost lovely, lying there, his black hair against the big, snow-white pillows. He was so relaxed and happy.

"Thaida," she whispered, "I have a big surprise for you."

He smiled and held her closely to him.

"You are so beautiful. Please tell me this great surprise."

She pulled out the photograph from inside her nightdress and held it up to him. He took it in his hand and looked closely at it. It was a long and serious look.

"That little beauty is ours. Yours and mine," she announced nervously.

He leapt up suddenly and, for a tense moment, she didn't know whether he was happy or angry. He was still scrutinising the photograph, his hands trembling.

"Yes! Yes! He is mine, he is my son, I see it. I know it. He is beautiful. My son is divine."

Then he paused and looked with urgency at Margaret Anne.

"But where is he? Where is my son? Why was I not told?"

"He's at home in Ireland. You see, Thaida, I was very ill, and I couldn't take care of him myself. My cousin is caring for him."

"At home is not Ireland," he said angrily. "At home is here with me -- his father -- and his mother."

"I know that, Thaida, I know. We'll get him. That's why I came to you."

"You will marry me then, Margaret Anne?" he asked lovingly. "And be a good mother to him?"

She threw herself into his arms.

"I will. Oh, I will! I do love you," she vowed falsely.

Her plan had worked like a dream. Her troubles were over now. That baby was turning out to be worth far more than his weight in gold.

The rush of these memories and the pills she had taken wearied Margaret Anne and she sank deeper into the huge bed. All there was to remember now was that second trip to Ireland. The trip with Thaida to take possession of their six-month-old baby. That same baby on whose face she'd refused to look after his birth and about whom she had felt no hesitation, but rather immense relief, in giving to her first cousin and his wife.

As if in some hazy dream, she could see the ashen, anguish-ridden face of her crippled cousin Gavin, sitting there in his wheelchair, bitterly resentful as he handed the child over. His little wife, a frail, insignificant-looking slip of a girl was somewhere in the kitchen.

"I know it is hard for you," Thaida had said, "but what can I do? I'm so sorry, but he is my son, and I love him even before I see him."

Later, after he'd seen little Georgie, Thaida had reached into the inside pocket of his dark grey coat and took out a cheque and handed it to Gavin.

"For you and your good wife," he'd said. "A token of my deep gratitude."

Gavin had taken the piece of paper and ripped it to pieces.

But it was all very vague now. At this moment, Margaret Anne was drifting into a deep sleep in the mansion on Pacific Boulevard. The pills were mercifully doing their trick.

Downstairs, however, in the huge lounge, sleep was the last thing on Thaida's mind.

"This is my baby, my son and heir," he said, his voice thick with pride.

He was addressing his three house staff as he held little Georgie lovingly and proudly in his chubby arms. Louise was overcome. The short, fat, middle-aged black housekeeper threw her hands up and in a voice alive with emotion exclaimed,"Mr Khan sir, but isn't he cute? I swear he the most adorable baby I ever did see. He look so like yourself. You the lucky man."

Thaida grinned from ear to ear.

But Ezra, his seventeen-year-old Indian houseboy, looked sad. He felt a twinge of envy at the love in his master's eyes for this infant.

"He's a lucky baby," Ezra said softly, not really meaning to be heard.

He had never known his own father and Mr Khan had always treated him like a son. Thaida was quick to detect the strong note of sadness in the boy's voice.

"You will take care of him as if you were his older brother," he said to Ezra. "You will love each other, and I will love you both."

He laid his hand on Ezra's shoulder.

Tyrone, Thaida's chauffeur and right-hand man, was less enthusiastic about this latest arrival. The poor old dude, he thought, he's gone soft on this kid. More of a nuisance than anything else, I guess. Still, no sense in rocking the boat.

"I'm happy for you, boss," he remarked diplomatically.

Little Georgie seemed frightened and bewildered as his big, brown eyes looked from one to another, scanning the scene to find a familiar face in these strange surroundings. He waved his arms about. They were nearly as brown as his father's. Thaida stroked him on the cheek in an effort to make him smile, but the baby's lower lip dropped and he began to cry fiercely. Thaida tried to soothe him, but only succeeded in making him yell the more loudly.

"Don't cry my son, Papa's here, and he'll take great care of his precious treasure. Hush now."

He squeezed the baby so tightly that Georgie's screams could be heard throughout the huge house. Louise couldn't stand it a moment longer, her strong maternal instincts surged forth.

"Come to Mamma Louise," she cried. "You tired and hungry, you poor little thing."

Thaida handed him over almost reverently, and she cuddled him gently and lovingly against her voluptuous breast. His little sobs ebbed away and his eyelids drooped in slumber. Thaida looked at him, adoring him.

"How peaceful he is now. You certainly have the touch, Louise. I will arrange for a nurse to take care of him as soon as I get a suitable one. We can't be too careful, can we?"

"You take your time Mr Khan. He'll be okay with Mamma Louise. I raised ten younguns of my own, didn't I?"

Tyrone was disgusted. This disruption in a well-run household wasn't at all to his liking. And from what he knew of the baby's mother she would be no help at all. In fact he was sure she'd be a great hindrance. Where was she now? That was a good question. She wasn't at all concerned for her son. Tyrone was roused from his musings by Thaida's snapping fingers.

"Come along to my study, Tyrone. There are some things to be done. This house has to be made ready for my son."

Tyrone threw his eyes up to heaven and followed his boss to the study.

"You come along also, Ezra. Tyrone will need some help."

Thaida seated himself on a brown, leather swivel chair behind a huge, mahogany desk. He opened a drawer and took out a gold telephone index, the rings on his fingers flashing as he searched for numbers.

"Ah yes, here we are, James Christopher Beatty, he will have the very best of nursery furniture."

He dialled Beatty's number and many others while Tyrone stood there impatiently shifting from one leg to another, chewing his gum with a vengeance. Ezra was lost in admiration at the magnificent array of paintings that lined almost every inch of the walls of this enormous room. He'd only been asked in on three other occasions. He didn't notice the chauffeur swearing under his breath, growing more frantic by the minute.

Was he ever going to stop ordering stuff? What was this foolishness that had come over him? It's that bitch, that conniving, scheming bitch. Finally everything was arranged.

"It's great to have friends in business," Thaida chuckled, handing Tyrone his instructions on a slip of paper. "Take the Mercedes van and pick up the essentials right away. Mr Beatty will have it ready for you -- the cot, play-pen and feeding chair. My son must have some kind of comfort."

CHAPTER 2

Margaret Anne opened her eyes. Night already. Her head pounded and her lips were dry. Desolate and disoriented, she struggled to her feet and made her way to the window. Her feet made no sound on the plush, gold carpet. She leaned through the opened window, allowing the cool night air to play on her face. But then she sensed something move in the darkness behind her, and she stifled back a shriek.

She whirled around in terror to see Thaida coming towards her, his eyes sparkling. My God, this is all I need, she thought as he took her in his arms and kissed her affectionately. "Are you all right my sweet? You look pale and tired."

She had to humour him. Besides she hadn't the strength or energy to struggle. And she needed this man. Or rather she needed his fat cheque book.

"I'm okay, darling, just a little tired and jet-lagged."

As she spoke her eyes flitted to the untouched cocaine on the locker beside her bed. She needed it now.

"Is everything to your taste, princess?" he asked tenderly. "You know I am yours to command. You have made me a very happy man giving me this wonderful son."

You stupid, old sugar daddy, she said to herself, responding outwardly with a smile which came only from her lips. "I'm so glad you feel that way, Ted."

Ted was his pet name and she knew he loved it when she called him that. He looked amorously into her eyes. Oh God, why can't he just go away and let me alone? She felt restless and enclosed, locked in his embrace. His shiny, white teeth, with the vulgar, gold fillings, grated on her nerves. In fact, everything about him now annoyed her intensely -- his happiness, his affection for her, his absolute insistence on running his hand constantly through her hair. She felt like screaming, but that would be a big mistake. She must act out the part of a woman in love. Oh, but God, tonight she just wasn't able. In desolation of spirit, she gently extricated herself from his arms. "Ted, I feel so dizzy tonight. I'm afraid I have to lie down, I'm so faint."

"You poor darling. Let me help you back to bed. I will have Louise send you up a tray."

"Oh no, you mustn't do that. I couldn't eat a thing. But a pot of coffee would be great, actually."

She waited for him to obey, but he didn't leave for the coffee. How long more would she have to play out this farce? He sat on the edge of the bed.

"You know my darling I have decided to change our son's name. I don't like that Georgie, it's not noble or genteel enough for him. I shall call him Bikram after my grandfather."

Margaret Anne couldn't care less what he called him. She wasn't even mildly interested in Thaida Khan, or in his son. "Yes, that's a much nicer name. I like it, I'm happy with it," she said with feigned enthusiasm.

"That's agreed then, and guess what I'm going to call you, my beauty?"

He was beaming now.

"I have no idea," she replied, her tone now slightly peeved.

This pretence was exhausting her. Thaida seemed not to notice, and continued.

"I will call you Marianna, my beautiful Marianna. Doesn't that sound more like you?"

"I guess it does."

In spite of herself she actually liked it. There was definitely a touch of class about it.

"And now tell me, when will we be married?" he asked.

That question sent shivers through every atom of her being. But she'd made a deal, and it would have to be carried through. "That's up to you, love. When you make the arrangements, I'm ready. But let's not discuss it tonight. I really don't feel up to it."

"Very well, princess, I will let you have your rest. And I will see you later."

There was a glint in his eye as he said this last that she emphatically didn't like. He definitely must not sleep in her bed tonight. She must find some way out of that. Her mind reached and schemed. "Oh Ted, by the way," she began casually, "there is an old wedding custom in Ireland."

"And what might that be, my sweet?"

"Well, the groom doesn't stay in the bride's bed until after the wedding, it's bad luck. And I wouldn't want anything to go wrong with our marriage. Would you?"

Thaida nodded thoughtfully, totally taken in by it. What a stupid old man he was.

"Of course not. It is very important that we are very happy. We must make our marriage work, and we must be good loving parents to Bikram. I will honour this tradition of your country and I will stay in the guest room with my son."

"I'm relieved that you see it that way, Ted."

Relieved is putting it mildly, she thought.

"But it won't be long before we tie the knot, and then you will be mine, all mine."

He kissed her gently and affectionately before he left the room.

"Ted and Marianna," she repeated aloud to herself over and over again. What an unlikely couple. But what possibilities, she thought, looking longingly at the white substance lined up on the little mirror behind the pale, green lamp. Suddenly, her reaching arm quivered. There was a knock on the door. "Who is it?"

"It's me -- Louise. I'm bringing your coffee, ma'am."

"Oh, come right in, Louise."

The woman ambled across the floor carrying a silver tray with two pots of steaming coffee.

"Put it on the table beside the window, Louise."

"Yes, ma'am," she said as she obeyed. "Will that be all, ma'am?" "Yes, thank you, Louise." But then, for the sake of appearances, she quickly added, "How is my son?"

The woman's eyes lit up.

"He just perfect, ma'am. Fed and washed up and fast asleep in his new, blue cot in the guest room. He so beautiful. I love him already, and Mr Khan, he just adore him."

"Thank you, Louise. I am sure he'll grow to love you too."

Louise was still beaming when she left the room. It's easy to please some folk, Margaret Anne thought. But then it takes all sorts, and feeding babies and changing diapers was definitely not for her. She turned the key in the bedroom door and quickly returned to the little mirror. This was for her. "Adieu, reality" she said, taking a deep sniff of coke. "Goodbye Margaret Anne, welcome Marianna."

Soon the moonlight made exquisite patterns on the wall. How beautiful. It was like a real-life kaleidoscope. What brilliant colours. She leapt out of bed. This is a perfect night. She looked at herself in the life-size mirror. Who is this magnificent young girl, so tall and slender, with such divine, blue eyes, such lustrous, blonde hair falling around her shoulders, bouncing when she moves? Marianna, such an elegant lady. And what a perfect name for this perfect specimen of humanity.

She twirled across the floor and opened the cabinet where Thaida kept compact discs. She flicked quickly through them. Madonna suited her mood tonight. She popped it into the player and, as she danced around the room, she thought that some day she would compose music herself and make her own records. She definitely had the musical talent. Marianna will one day be famous, just like Madonna. The very thought of it made her heart beat rapidly with excitement. The more she contemplated it, the more real it became. Marianna would soon, very soon, be a huge international star. She had what it took. She could visualise it all quite clearly now. Her first hit single, number one in the charts, her picture on millions of singles and CDs, the press conferences, world tours, the constant round of glittering parties, the thousands of fans crowding around to get her autograph.

She'd need a manager of course, and a very good one. It would have to be someone energetic, who knew the business, had good contacts, and who could really sell her and her music. Her mind raced. Then it came to her. I have him, of course. Gordon Edwards of Star Enterprises, the very man.

She lit a cigarette, and as she smoked it the image of Gordon, long at the back of her mind, re-emerged -- his blonde good looks, his perfect manners, the finesse with which he operated. When she'd worked for him he had always said that she was the most attractive girl in the office.

She rooted in her handbag for her diary and found his number. There was a time when she had it off by heart, she recalled, dialling.

The phone beside Gordon's bed buzzed several times before he finally awakened. He picked it up and glanced at his watch.

"Yes, who is it?"

"Hi, Gordon. Guess who? It's me, Margaret Anne."

There was a moment of silence, then it registered.

"Oh, it's you, Mags. What on earth is the problem?"

He hadn't expected to hear from Mags O'Dowd again. At one point he thought there could be something between them, but he'd given up those thoughts. She was far too wild for him. But somehow her voice still stirred something deep inside him.

"Problem? No problem at all. I was just wondering if you would be my manager?"

Gordon didn't believe what he was hearing.

"Mags, do you know what time it is?"

"Haven't a clue. Who cares about time? There's plenty of it anyway."

"So, it's four in the morning, and you're calling to ask me to be your manager?"

"You got it."

She's stoned out of her little mind. There was no point in talking to her now.

"Call me tomorrow. I'll sleep on it," he said, hanging up.

But he couldn't return to sleep. He just tossed and turned, and couldn't get her out of his mind. To be her manager, that's what she wants. What was she about to do? She was a clever, strong-willed and very attractive girl. She'd been great at the agency until her crazy lifestyle affected her work. He'd had no choice but to let her go. Whatever she was about to become he was certain she would succeed at it. She had always succeeded in landing the very large accounts when she put her mind to it. Managing Margaret Anne, yes, he liked it. It would definitely be a challenge.

Meanwhile, inspired, Margaret Anne put pen to paper and began to compose the lyrics for her first song. The words and ideas flowed from her. She couldn't get them down fast enough. It was as though she were outside of herself and someone else was pouring the beautiful words out. She didn't hear the knocking on the door for quite some time. Then she heard Thaida's voice.

"Are you awake, my Marianna?"

"Be with you in a sec," she called as she quickly and carefully put the cocaine back into the locker. That out of the way, she opened the door.

Thaida eyed her curiously and glanced around the room at the sheer untidiness of it -- the coffee pot overturned on the floor amid records, compact discs, dirty ashtrays, cigarette packs, and sheet upon sheet of paper.

"What have you been up to?" he asked in amazement.

She must appease him now, he was vital to all her plans. She flew into his arms.

"I couldn't sleep, love, so guess what, I decided to write a song."

He was smiling now.

"And did you write it?" he asked.

"I did indeed," she proudly answered. She then took the piece of paper she'd been working on from the pocket of her dressing gown and read a few lines of it to him.

As I traverse this dreary planet
seeking happiness and peace,
all I find is desolation,
why is there never ease?

My spirit is dejected
as I wander near and far
seeking something that I know
I'll only find beyond a star

Thaida was very impressed.

"But they're such beautiful, such divine sentiments. You are a genius, my Marianna."

"Oh thanks, Ted," she replied, kissing him affectionately. "I must put music to it now."

"I look forward to the finished product," he said, and then his expression became serious again.

"Marianna," he began, "I have terrible news for you, my sweet. I have trouble in my restaurant in San Francisco. The head chef is causing problems. More money, that's what he wants. It's always the same -- more and more money for less and less work. I have to fly there this morning to sort things out. I may be back tonight if all goes well, but I will call to let you know at any rate."

This was music to her ears.

"I'm so sorry my love, but of course I'll be okay. I'll be waiting for your call. And I do hope things work out for you."

As he was about to leave the room she spoke as if she'd just remembered something.

"Oh Ted, by the way, I need some clothes and other bits and pieces. And, well, I haven't a cent."

"Ah, but we must do something about that."

He opened his wallet and counted out five hundred dollars. "That should be enough for the moment, until I get a chance to arrange some credit cards for you. I will call Monique now before I go. She will have the finest of clothes. You know where her boutique is, don't you? Monique's in Segunda Street. Tyrone will take you there, and you may get anything you require. I will have an account set up for you right away."

"Oh thank you, love. I do love you, Ted."

"My wife will always have the very best."

His wife. The sting is in the tail. It doesn't bear thinking of, she told herself as he left the room.

CHAPTER 3

Monique emerged from behind the counter of the glamorous boutique, gesticulating and gabbling frantically. She was a beautiful woman, in her forties perhaps, with sallow skin, and ebony hair swept up in a bun tied with a large, white bow.

"I'm afraid my French is rather scant," Margaret Anne remarked. Monique apologised and switched to heavily accented English.

"Mr Khan told me you were coming. He described you very well, ma belle."

"Did he?" Margaret Anne replied casually as her eyes scanned the rails and rails laden with glorious garments.

"I see you're anxious to get down to business," Monique remarked.

She now faced a wonderful opportunity as a businesswoman and fashion expert. She could make a month's profit on this account alone if she played her cards well and used her expertise to the full. She quickly picked some garments from the rails.

"The line must be long, ma belle, always long. This suit, that blouse, and ooh la la, this cocktail dress. Try them on, please."

The colours didn't lose their lustre even in the harsh light of the changing-room. Margaret Anne slipped into the heavy, peacock-blue, silk blouse, a little alarmed at the plunging neckline. Nervously, she stepped outside.

"Mon dieu, but it's beautiful ma belle, why hide it?" Monique gushed, reaching forward and drawing down Margaret Anne's arms to her side.

Margaret Anne smiled a little, mischievous smile and then went back into the changing-room. She donned the cream suit with the pencil skirt and very long jacket.

"Très magnifique."

Monique was in raptures, and Margaret Anne herself was quite pleased with the reflection she saw in the mirror.

"And now the cocktail dress, try this s'il vous plaît," Monique said, proffering a luxurious dress in dark red.

There wasn't much material in it, it looked so skimpy, but when Margaret Anne paraded around the shop wearing it to perfection she knew it was a masterpiece.

"So beautiful, so subtle," Monique purred. "You are a pleasure to dress."

Monique plucked more clothes from the rails, giving a running commentary on their beauty and elegance, all the while convincing her young customer how wonderful she looked in each of the creations. Her flattery achieved its purpose. Soon the counter was cluttered with dresses, blouses, and very chic hats and scarves. The white, leather suit was the pièce de resistance, and Margaret Anne decided to wear it home.

Tyrone arrived just when she needed him.

"How do I look?" she asked, pivoting around the shop.

"Seen worse," Tyrone mumbled grudgingly, seething with anger.

He couldn't tolerate such a spoiled, selfish bitch as this one. He carried the bags and boxes roughly out to the waiting Rolls.

"Envy will get you nowhere," Margaret Anne quipped as she stepped haughtily into the back seat.

"To Oak Trees Avenue, Chula Vista, please," she ordered. "I want to visit my parents."

Tyrone had no choice but to obey. As they drove, his anger mounted, and he feared he would lose control. He had a violent temper, and if he let go he would end up in trouble himself. He turned the radio on to take his mind off his hateful passenger. The phone in the car trilled.

"Yes, boss," Tyrone replied. "I'll put her on to you right away. Mr Khan for you," he said, abruptly handing her the telephone.

"Hi, Ted."

"Hello, my darling. How did the shopping go?"

"Just wonderful. I'm so excited. I can't wait to dress up for you."

"Nor can I wait to see you, but unfortunately I have not yet succeeded in sorting out Pierre, so I will not be home until sometime tomorrow night. I'm missing you."

"Me too," she lied.

"But absence makes the heart grow fonder."

"What a sweet thing to say. I love you."

Some minutes later Tyrone stopped the car outside her parents house.

"Come back in a few hours," she said, and as she was about to get out she pointed to the boxes and bags.

"Put those things in my room, and mind you don't steal anything."

He gritted his teeth, revved up the car violently, and drove off.

Eoin and Gráinne were sitting together in the kitchen having lunch. There was silence between them, but it was a peaceful, harmonious kind of silence, one they often shared when they knew words were not necessary to communicate their feelings. Gráinne sipped her tea and thought idly to herself what life would be like without Eoin. He was always there for her, always attentive to her demands, always patient with her sad moods, which were quite frequent lately with all her daughter's antics. It was Eoin who gave the true meaning to her life, especially since their daughter had left home. Margaret Anne was a constant worry to them. Gráinne was so glad Eoin had decided to take these few days off. She needed him like the air she breathed. He was her rock, the very core of her life. She was roused from her musings by the ring on the door bell.

"Who could this be?" she asked as Eoin got up to answer it.

They were both very happy to see Margaret Anne.

"Think of an angel," her mother said.

"Would you believe that I was just now thinking about you?"

She came to the door and embraced Margaret Anne lovingly.

"You look very glamorous today," Eoin remarked.

"That's a beautiful suit."

"Pure leather too," Margaret Anne said, holding out a sleeve for her mother to feel the texture.

"It's absolutely divine. It must have cost a fortune."

"It cost me nothing, not even a cent. Thaida bought it for me and lots more besides."

Gráinne and Eoin looked questioningly at each other.

"Is that Georgie's father?" Eoin asked at last.

"Yes, but he's now called 'Bikram'. Thaida didn't think that 'Georgie' was aristocratic enough for his son."

Gráinne couldn't stop herself from speaking.

"Do you intend to marry this man?" she asked hesitantly.

"As a matter of fact, yes. And quite soon, in fact. I'm inviting you both to the wedding."

"Is he a Catholic?" Gráinne dared to ask.

Margaret Anne threw her eyes up to heaven.

"Typical Irish mother's question. How brainwashed you all are."

Eoin quickly interjected.

"Your mother is just asking a perfectly normal question. After all you were brought up in the Catholic religion."

Margaret Anne was irritable and argumentative now.

"The answer to your question is no, he is not a Catholic, and I don't know what he is. But the only religion I'm interested in is a large bank account, and he sure has that."

Eoin placed his arms around Gráinne. He knew this would upset her. Just when she was beginning to be herself again after a long bout of depression. He also knew that there was little or no point in arguing with his daughter.

"If that's the way you feel, then off you go. But I sincerely hope you won't be sorry," he said.

"Will it be a church wedding?" Gráinne asked, her voice trembling.

"No mum, we will just go to the nearest registry office and legalise our union. This is America, you know, and it is the twentieth century."

Gráinne's voice suddenly found some vigour.

"Don't expect your father or myself to be there. We won't have hand, act, nor part in it. I'm thoroughly ashamed of you, Margaret Anne."

Margaret Anne's eyes flashed with anger now. She felt like screaming, or throwing something at her parents, but instead she twirled, wrenched open the door, and stormed out. Then just as abruptly she popped her head back inside.

"You know, I pity the two of you poor fools. You were never in the real world, that's your problem. Constantly hiding behind Mother Church. So I'll leave you to lament your wayward daughter. God bless old Ireland," she shouted mockingly and laughed aloud a bitter, sarcastic laugh as she slammed the door.

Gráinne collapsed into sobs and Eoin took her gently in his arms.

"Where did we go wrong?" she repeated over and over again. "We should never have brought her to this country."

"There's no point in recriminations," Eoin soothed her.

"And I don't think we did go wrong. We brought her up to behave correctly and we tried to instil good morals, values, and attitudes. I don't think we could have done anymore. We were always extremely helpful to her and we tried at all times to solve any problems she had."

Eoin's voice was soothing and eventually Gráinne grew quiet and thoughtful.

"We may have been too helpful, and maybe we made her over-dependent so that she felt incompetent and inadequate. Perhaps that was what made her take drugs. Or maybe I didn't openly express my love and affection for her."

She dissolved into tears again and Eoin couldn't find the words to console her. His own heart was breaking but he had to be strong for her.

"Come on now, darling, you know we did our very best. Guilt is a useless sentiment and only leads nowhere. Let's trust the good Lord and put her in His care, we can't do any more. Sure, didn't I often hear my mother say that nothing is impossible to God? Cheer up now, and I'll make you a nice cup of tea."

As they both sat at the little, oak table and sipped the tea the special bulletin on the television quickly took their focus off their daughter. An earthquake measuring seven on the Richter Scale had shaken San Francisco. It was believed that over two hundred people had been killed and many more injured. Gráinne's face became pale as death. Eoin had never seen her so shocked and frightened.

"My God, what a terrible tragedy. I'm scared Eoin."

"It's a dreadful disaster, and God help the families of the dead. But don't be afraid, it's all over now. We may get some aftershocks, but even if we do there's no need to worry. There are strict earthquake-proof building codes here now. Sure, even the skyscrapers are designed so that they can sway and absorb the earthquake's energy."

"How were all these people killed then?" she asked nervously.

"Oh, they must have been trapped in old buildings or something."

"I wish we could go back to Ireland. It's the best little country in the world."

Meanwhile Margaret Anne had made her way to Freddie's Hideout, a plush, cosy cocktail bar at the end of the road. Freddie's had been her favourite haunt when she'd worked at Star Enterprises. Tonight she sat in an alcove with some friends she hadn't met for quite some time. They smoked joints and swallowed back Bloody Marys until they were as high as kites. The buzz was exhilarating. She had made her connection earlier and had a huge quantity of snow stashed in her leather shoulder bag.

Gordon Edwards came in and heard her before he saw her.

"Hi, you dope fiends," he said as he sat down at the table. "What are you celebrating?"

"Life," Margaret Anne exclaimed aloud.

"Wonderful life and a wonderful world."

Gordon knew she was totally spaced out. He wondered if she even remembered calling him. He leaned forward and spoke gently.

"Haven't you heard about the earthquake?"

"Earthquake?" she said. "Who cares about earthquakes?"

She laughed aloud until tears rolled down her cheeks. Gordon felt ill at ease now and watched her closely. She had certainly gone on some trip. He had better make an effort to get her home before she cracked up completely. He stood up, took her hand in his, and pulled her to her feet.

"Come on, Mags," he said, "let's go."

Laying his arm around her waist, he guided her towards the door. In the parking lot he bundled her into his car and drove off.

"Not to my parents house!" she shouted. "I live with Thaida Khan now."

Gordon was unsettled by this information. Margaret Anne, meanwhile, jabbered incoherently for the rest of the trip. She was talking in riddles and her speech was slurred, so that Gordon couldn't understand a word she said. He reached Pacific Boulevard, where he knew Khan lived. After pulling in, he escorted her to the door. He rang the bell, went back to his car, and waited until the door was opened and he saw that she was safely inside. Ezra was shocked when he saw her.

"Where's Ted," she asked in a sullen voice.

"Tyrone went to the airport to pick him up. But he just phoned to say there are no flights from San Francisco. Mr Khan must be staying there until things are back to normal."

Pleased, Margaret Anne headed towards the stairs and staggered.

"Shall I help you ma'am?" Ezra asked.

Suddenly she glared at him.

"Get out of my way you little bastard," she heard herself hiss.

Ezra ran into the kitchen to tell Louise. Margaret Anne's progress up the stairs was so slow that she heard Louise's response.

"Pay her no heed, boy. She an evil woman. I pity poor Mr Khan and little Bikram."

CHAPTER 4

Margaret Anne stretched under the pink, satin sheet and moaned as the horrible effects of the night before sent acute pain drumming through her head. Sleepily she glanced around the room and, in spite of the drawn curtains, she could see the sunlight flooding through. It must be quite late, she realised as she struggled out of bed and looked at her watch.

It was eleven-thirty. She was surprised Thaida hadn't wakened her. Almost by reflex, she opened the locker. Her heart sank to find not a speck of coke left on the little mirror. As panic started to spread in her throat she suddenly remembered. Yes, she'd made her connection last night. And there was her stash, wrapped neatly in her little leather bag. After a long and prolonged snort, she got up and drew open the rose-coloured curtains. The street seemed like a scene from a movie, all brilliant colour and light, with so much noise and movement. Feeling hot and dizzy, she decided to take a shower.

A little less than fifteen minutes later she paraded into the large, red-and-white kitchen, looking as fresh as a daisy in the lime-green tracksuit, one of Monique's creations. She was taken aback by the scene that confronted her there.

Louise stood beside the cooker in a fit of hysterical crying. She barely glanced up from her heaving sobs at Margaret Anne's entrance. Tyrone openly glared at her and then sat down at the round, red table beside an apparently broken-hearted Ezra. The trembling boy cradled a mug of coffee in his hands as large tears flowed hopelessly down his bronze face. Little Bikram gurgled at her from his feeding chair waving a well-chewed rusk in his little, messy hands.

"What the hell is wrong with everybody? This place is like a funeral parlour."

"You got that right," Louise blubbered and wiped her eyes with her pure-white apron.

"Master Khan is dead, he dead, dead."

Margaret Anne took a half-step back, shocked.

"What happened to him?" she managed to ask.

Tyrone replied in a tone that exuded hatred and disdain, "You probably don't know, but there was an earthquake in San Francisco."

"Oh God," she exclaimed, putting her hands to her mouth. "You surely don't mean that Mr. ..."

"Yes," Tyrone said in a surprisingly soft voice.

"He was trapped in his car when the Cypress Freeway collapsed. His brother already went and identified the body. He'll be here tomorrow. He's in charge of all the boss's business now."

By the end, Tyrone's voice had regained its rancour, and he even laughed sarcastically at the mention of the boss's business. Margaret Anne swallowed. Clearly she was considered a piece of that business.

"Lord help us all, this is a bad tragedy," Louise wailed.

Ezra also began to blubber loudly. Margaret Anne, however, was reduced to silence for a few minutes. But when the initial shock passed she was swept over by a surge of relief. Saved by the bell. She wouldn't have to go through with this dreaded marriage after all. Then panic gripped her. How was she to survive? She couldn't face life without drugs, and money was vital. And without Thaida both of these necessities would dry up. Then from somewhere in the depths of her subconscious mind a twinge of sadness emerged. Poor old Ted. He was such a kind, gentle and generous soul. She must have had some slight fondness for him after all.

"What am I to do, Tyrone?"

She tried to cry but not a single tear would come.

"How should I know?" he retorted sharply.

"Just don't forget to take your baby with you. He needs a good mother like you."

She was furious. That black bastard. He could always touch a nerve in her.

"How dare you speak to me like that? I am not cut out to be a mother. I have other things to do."

"It looks like you don't have much choice now, do you?"

"We'll soon see," she replied defiantly, and then, raising her voice and addressing all three of them, she said, "Get off your butts and do what you're paid to do. A little less fake mourning and a little more real work. I'm starving."

With brutal swiftness Tyrone jumped up from the chair and caught her by the hair. She whimpered as he tugged her roughly to the door and flung her towards the stairs.

"Get the hell out of here you cold, selfish bitch. You'll be out on your ass tomorrow, you can count on that."

"You dirty black animal," she screamed when she'd regained her balance and her breath.

"I'll see that you get what you deserve."

She scampered up the stairs and locked her door, gritting her teeth in anger. When she had cooled down a little, images ran through her mind at the speed of light. Curled up on the bed, she tried to plan some strategy. She must make an impression on Thaida's brother. And little Bikram would once again be her trump card.

CHAPTER 5

Thaida's brother, Jonathan Khan, spotted Margaret Anne at once. She sat on a large, peach-coloured rocking chair at the far end of the living room, just beside the French doors which led out to the veranda. She held her baby in her arms and looked so lost, so alone. His heart melted. He could see why his brother loved this woman and her beautiful brown baby. He had been afraid the baby would be white. But no, he was a rich, deep brown. Oh, how he would love a son like that. His wife had given him only daughters. Alone in the world now, mother and son made a sad, sorry sight. He hesitated on the threshold for a moment before going in, looking intently at them. She was certainly beautiful for a white woman. And the boy looked so much like Thaida he wanted to cry. A very difficult and sensitive situation awaited him.

Then suddenly she glanced up, rose, and walked towards him.

"You must be Jonathan," she said.

"Yes. Thaida has spoken a lot to me about you, but I am so sorry that we have to meet under such tragic circumstances. It's very sad indeed, but then life has no mercy," he said, stroking his little nephew on the face.

"What a beautiful baby. He must be a great joy to you now, a loving reminder of Thaida."

"Sometimes I think he may bring back his memory too vividly," she said in a very soft voice, looking lovingly at Bikram.

"Gosh, he's heavy," she added and leaned forward and gently lowered him into his play-pen. They both sat down. There were a few moments of silence as they stared at each other, weighing each other up.

She was certainly a very striking woman, dressed to perfection in an elegant, black, silk dress that screamed money. It was her large, blue eyes that held him most. Such exquisite eyes, they seemed like two bottomless, blue pools.

She had heard quite a lot about him, but she hadn't expected him to be so suave and good looking. His jet-black hair, parted in the centre, was like woven silk, and he was impeccably groomed and expensively dressed.

"What do you plan to do now?" he asked at last in a kindly, though curious tone of voice. This was the question she had been waiting for and she had her answer well rehearsed.

"Well, Jonathan," she began, casting her eyes downwards, "I gave up an excellent job in an advertising agency when I discovered I was pregnant, and I returned to Ireland some months before Bikram's birth. You see, I wanted to be sure that I would give Thaida a strong, healthy baby. I raised him myself for the first six months of his life. And as you can see, he got the very best of care and attention."

She shook a rattle and cooed and little Bikram lurched over to the side of his play-pen and laughed happily at his mother.

"Oh yes, that is quite obvious, he is a credit to you, my dear."

She laughed an ironic, weak, little laugh and then cast her eyes down and continued.

"But he's not a great credit to my bank account, as you can imagine. The fact is, Jonathan, that now I'm broke. Thaida was about to arrange a line of credit for me."

Jonathan coughed nervously. She was looking for money. She was expecting him to give her money before she took this princely child away.

"I may as well be frank with you, Margaret Anne. My brother's affairs are in a horrible mess. He expanded too rapidly and lived too extravagantly. And well, the bottom line is that all his assets, including this house, will have to be sold and there may not even be enough to cover his liabilities."

Margaret Anne's jaw dropped. She was shocked to the core and Jonathan could see it clearly. Her face became as pale as death and she was reduced to silent panic. Her plan had crumbled like a large sand castle.

"I have given the staff three months pay to help them until they get other jobs," Jonathan continued. "And it was Thaida's wish that Ezra should come to live with me."

"And what about my son and the mother who bore him? Where do we fit into things?" Margaret Anne asked sharply, ignoring Bikram who had started to cry.

A curious unease took hold of Jonathan. Was this woman angling after something besides money?

"Forgive me, but Thaida left no clear wishes regarding you and your son. You reappeared in his life rather suddenly, you see. Do you anticipate difficulty in keeping the child?"

"I can't afford to keep myself, never mind a child."

"You mean you'd give him up?"

"I've got to think about myself first," she replied icily. "And I wouldn't know how to change a diaper."

When she spoke she glared with annoyance at the baby. It then struck Jonathan that this woman was not after money for herself and her magnificent son. She was after money for herself only. As impossible as it was to believe, this woman seemed to care nothing for her noble son. Now that she'd seen Thaida's money was gone she wanted to be rid of his son as well. Fury welled up within Jonathan, but he kept himself outwardly composed.

"There is no need to upset yourself," he said, keeping his voice calm.

"Little Bikram will be well looked after. My wife and I would treasure him. If that is what you wish."

"You will, of course, give me a substantial sum of money to keep myself until I get a job."

This bitch is trying to sell me this boy. My own brother's son! He is mine by rights. He will carry on the great Khan name. Jonathan's thoughts were in turmoil, but as always, he prided himself on his unruffled exterior.

"How much are you talking about?"

"I would require ten thousand dollars, at least."

He was taken aback by this demand, but on quick reflection he thought of the infant. How could she treat such a noble looking infant with such disdain? Though he was stretched to his very limits with his own debts, not to mention those of his brother, he would pay her her money. That was the only way to get Bikram away from her terrible clutches immediately. But he would not forget what she was doing. He would not let her get away with putting a price on what was so obviously meant to be his. This woman would pay for the humiliation she put upon his heir. She would live to regret this day. "I will give you a cheque for that amount, but first you will come to my attorney and sign some documents. There can only be one payment, you understand?"

"I understand," she said, trying to keep herself from smiling, wishing he would take the bawling, black baby and be gone.

"I'll pick you up at two-thirty tomorrow. Bring Bikram." And the conversation came to an abrupt end as he turned and left the room.

CHAPTER 6

Margaret Anne awakened feeling as weak and ill as someone in the throes of a very severe flu. Her whole body ached, and her head throbbed. Sometime before noon her mother came in and drew the curtains. Light flooded in and stabbed at her eyes, blinding her. She tried to lift her head but it was as heavy as lead. Oh God, oh God, she said to herself, I'm dying, let me die, oh please, let me die.

Gráinne peered down at her daughter, her expression a mixture of compassion and fear.

"You look awful, Margaret Anne. Are you all right? Can I get you anything?"

"Mineral water and lots of ice," she muttered faintly.

She wanted to close her eyes and sleep again, but she was terrified that at any moment now her skin would begin to move, to slither. All at once she wanted to burrow back into the lovely cocoon from which she had emerged, in which she felt no pain, no sorrow, no blackness, no hurt, nothing at all. One small fix would get her through this torturous hour. But then she'd made a deal with Gordon. And for some strange reason, unknown even to herself, this was one deal she was determined to keep. He said it would be difficult but it would be worth it. God, he was right about the difficult part anyway.

Her mother returned with a large glass jug of sparkling water and an ice pack which she lay across her forehead.

"Oh that feels better," Margaret Anne murmured. Gathering her strength, she sat up and gulped down the water until she could feel its coolness seeping through her entire being. She managed to sleep again for a while and she awoke to hear the phone beside her bed ring. She sat up with a start and felt quite dizzy. She groped for the yellow receiver, nearly knocking the phone off the bed table.

"Hello," she said sleepily.

"Good afternoon, sleepy head."

It was Gordon's voice.

"I thought you would be just about awake around now. How did you sleep?"

"Well enough," she replied. "But now I feel awful. God, will I ever go through with this?"

"Of course you will. We'll just take it day by day. Remember we're in this together, you and I, and we are going to kick it."

"Okay," she replied weakly, trying really to believe it herself. "But what do I do now?"

"You just get up, have a nice hot shower, put on your make-up, and dress in something pretty. Then relax over a cup of coffee and I'll be at the door in about an hour. We're going to have lunch."

"Oh no, Gordon, I couldn't eat a thing."

"Not to worry, I know exactly how you feel. But I also know the very thing that will tempt your delicate palate."

Gordon put the phone down and glanced at his watch; there was just enough time to complete the report on his desk, and he got down to it with gusto. The meeting with the computing firm had gone well, he felt. He and the agency had done their best. But he was far more pleased with what he was undertaking with Margaret Anne. So far so good, he thought. But there is a long, uphill struggle yet. But if I made it, so can she. Gordon shook his head, remembering the stupid things he'd done, and the stupid relationship he'd gotten into. Well, it was all over. His life was back on track thanks mainly to Charlie. And Charlie had always said to pay him back by helping someone else out. Here was his chance. It would be challenging and Gordon loved a challenge. It felt good to have a sense of purpose.

At two o'clock on the dot, Gordon hurried up the pathway to Margaret Anne's house. Gráinne answered the doorbell. She was surprised, and indeed very much relieved, to see a decent, respectable, good-looking man calling for her daughter.

"You must be Mrs O'Dowd," he said, shaking her hand warmly. "Although you look so young, you could be Mags's sister. I'm Gordon, a good friend of hers, we used to work together."

Gráinne was delighted with the compliment and his polite manner.

"Lovely to meet you, Gordon. You must have kissed the Blarney Stone at some stage," she remarked jovially as she led him in.

Margaret Anne stood in front of the fireplace in the lounge, eyeing her black skirt, waiting nervously. She looked tired but the colour black suited her perfectly, and the shimmering, beige blouse blended well with the creaminess of her delicate skin. Gordon had never seen her with her blonde hair swept up and he loved the ornate, black bandeaux. She walked towards him, half smiling, and he kissed her on the cheek.

"You look great."

"I wish I felt that way. I presume you introduced yourself to Mum."

He'd been so captivated by Margaret Anne's appearance that he'd completely forgotten about Gráinne's presence. Embarrassed, he turned around quickly to try to make up for this gaffe. But Gráinne herself was staring blankly out the window, lost in thought.

It was such a change, such an immense relief, to see Margaret Anne with a nice young man after all the weird undesirables she had known. Gráinne remembered the hurt when Margaret Anne had told her that she had no idea who the father of her child was, and that she really didn't want to know.

"Oh yes," Gordon said, bringing Gráinne's attention back to the room. "Your sister and I met at the door."

"He always says the right things," Margaret Anne said, eyeing him with pride.

As Gráinne told her daughter how delighted she was to see her bringing in friends like Gordon, Gordon himself glanced modestly around the room. It was delightful -- the warm, rose-coloured walls, the delicate, pink lamps scattered intermittently on mahogany occasional tables, and the most welcoming, comfortable, cream-coloured three-piece suite that he had ever seen. A little, red lamp in the alcove caught his eye and he noticed the picture of the Sacred Heart.

"There's something you won't see very often in this country," he said, pointing towards it.

"My mother in Ireland has great devotion to the Sacred Heart," Gráinne said simply. "And she instilled it into all three of her daughters."

"Well, actually," he continued, "we have exactly the same picture in our living room. You see my mother is also Irish, from Tipperary in fact. She emigrated when she was twenty and met my father in this country. He is very English and not of my mother's religious persuasion."

Margaret Anne was getting edgy now. When religion came up for discussion, it was time for her to go. It had always been a very contentious issue between her mother and herself.

"We better get rolling. It will be time to come home before we get out," she said, and taking Gordon by the arm, led him to the door.

"Have a nice lunch," Gráinne called.

"We sure will," Gordon replied, giving her a little peck on the cheek.

She was actually blushing as she went into the kitchen to catch up on her chores.

They drove about fifteen miles down the freeway and stopped at Ricardo's, a cosy, dimly-lit restaurant. A table was already booked and the rotund, oily-looking Mexican waiter led them to a quiet alcove and graciously seated them. He then lifted a bottle of champagne from a bucket of ice and opened it skillfully, before filling their glasses. Then, with a bow and a very broad beam that displayed a mouthful of white teeth, he left them.

Gordon raised his glass.

"Here's to a very beautiful and courageous lady."

Margaret Anne lifted her glass and smiled coyly.

"And to her most wonderful manager."

As their glasses met with a gentle clink, she suddenly suspected that she might be falling in love with this man. She was startled at this thought. She'd always told herself that men were to be used and not loved. She wasn't quite sure whether she liked this change that was taking place within her.

Gordon caught a glimpse of the waiter approaching with the meal he'd ordered ahead of time and said quickly, "Close your eyes now, and don't open them until I tell you."

Margaret Anne obeyed instantly like someone hypnotised. And as the plate was placed in front of her, the delicious aroma wafted up to her.

"Open now," he said, and when she did she was looking at a huge, oval plate of spare ribs in barbecue sauce.

"Oh my God, I'll never get through this cow," she exclaimed.

"Would you care to place a bet on that?"

"That would be easy money for me."

"We'll see," Gordon said amiably.

Margaret Anne watched as he tucked the little, white serviette in through the neck of his shirt and began to eat with relish, sucking his fingers at regular intervals. Margaret Anne followed suit, and as she nibbled the sumptuous meat she was soon left with a plate full of bare bones.

"What did I tell you?" he asked triumphantly.

"Right again," she agreed as she dipped her fingers in the bowl of water placed on the table for just that purpose.

At the coffee he noticed her hands were shaking. In fact, throughout the meal Gordon had quietly and discreetly studied her behaviour. It was patently obvious that she was agitated but he also knew that she was fighting hard.

"How are you feeling now?" he asked.

She lit a cigarette and did not reply for a moment.

"It's difficult to explain. I'm okay when I'm with you, I feel so safe and secure. But I'm scared of being alone. I don't trust myself, not really."

"But you can trust me, and I've already told you that I'll be available for you any time, day or night, for the next few months."

The next few months, she repeated silently in her mind. But it was the thought of living without him at the end of that time that frightened her. She shifted uneasily in her chair and Gordon detected the frown on her pretty face.

"Have I said something wrong?" he asked.

She laughed a little false, nervous laugh.

"God no," she replied, and moved her chair around the table so she was right next to him.

"It's just that I can't stand going home to my parents. They bore me intensely. They're so proper and righteous. And as for Dad, he drives me crazy, fussing about Mum all the time. I feel so isolated."

By now she had rested her hand on his knee and had steadily moved it up his thigh. Gordon was tempted, very tempted. But he knew it would be unfair to enter a physical relationship with her while she was yet so unstable and vulnerable. He realised he was acting as a crutch for her right now. And he knew from bitter experience that that was the worst possible basis for a relationship.

"I understand how you feel," he said, taking her hand firmly from his thigh. "But it will soon pass. You know, Mags, you've got everything going for you. You're a beautiful woman, bubbling over with personality. And you're extremely talented, and efficient and capable. I'm sorry you won't come back to Star. But when you're well again you'll have no problem picking up the threads of your life."

"It's so much easier for people like you. I don't know where to begin looking for a suitable job."

A thought suddenly triggered in Gordon's mind and he snapped his fingers excitedly.

"I might have the very job for you."

"Oh, you might, might you?" she replied with some enthusiasm.

"Well," he began, "I do quite a lot of promotional stuff for Ron Harte, the Programme Controller of Gold FM."

"The Irish radio station in San Diego?"

"That's the one. I've just remembered that someone's leaving in a month and he's looking for a jock."

"You mean a deejay, me a deejay?"

"Yes, you. I think you would be admirably suited to the role, the way you talk so much."

"Watch it, Gordon," she smiled.

"And, who knows, it could be your first step on the road to stardom."

"You know something? I like it. When can I start?"

"Hold on, take it easy, baby. We've still got to get you really straightened out first."

But I'd be happier doing something. I'll go crazy hanging around."

"Tell you what, why don't we get you to make a demo tape? I'll write you a nice script and I'll give you my Superscope to record on. You can spend the rest of the week practising until you get it perfect. In the meantime I'll talk to Ron and arrange an interview for you. How about that?"

Margaret Anne felt totally transformed.

"Thank you so much, Gordon," she gushed, throwing her arms around him.

But now, romance was the furthest thing from her mind. She threw herself into preparing for a radio career over the next several weeks. And they were some of the hardest weeks in her life. Many times she was on the verge of succumbing and getting high, but every time she felt like that, no matter what time it was, she called Gordon. He either talked her out of it on the phone or came over right away to see her through it. The dream of working at the radio station gave her something else to focus on. She read books, studied diction, practised for hours upon hours. As the time for the interview neared, she knew, no matter what happened, that she'd made it. She was a new woman.

CHAPTER 7

Six months later the name Mags O'Dowd, by which Margaret Anne was now known, was a household word in San Diego and the surrounding area.

She took to the microphone and the headphones like a duck to water and her exhilarating chit chat and lively repartee made her beloved of her listeners. Ron Harte was thrilled with his new-found star.

"She's a real favourite -- a professional performer, and the public worship her," he boasted to Gordon.

"I knew she'd be right for the job. That kid makes a go of everything she tries. She's got what it takes."

"You were bang on there, Gordon. I owe you one. Do you realise the ratings on her show have gone up to thirty-five per cent?"

"Great stuff," replied Gordon, feeling very proud. "Hey, keep an eye on her for me, will you, Ron? I don't see too much of her now, and we don't want her to relapse into her old ways and ruin everything do we?"

"You're dead right -- we don't. I'll keep watch for any tell-tale signs and I'll be in touch."

Ron definitely didn't want her to relapse into her old ways. The public loved her stories about growing up with Irish parents, the tales she told of Irish relatives, the high-spirited way she made light of everything. Despite her past, the image she projected on air was good-humoured, almost wholesome. She was lively and vivacious, but never raunchy or risqué. Young and old alike loved her. Ron Harte knew he'd have to protect this image. He'd have to do all he could to keep her off the drugs, not so much for Gordon, but for his station's ratings.

Margaret Anne, however, didn't need coke now to create a high, euphoric state within herself. Not with the constant adulation she received during live phone-ins, and the sacks of fan mail. People even recognised her on the street. She was on a beautiful ego trip. As word about the dynamic new deejay spread, newspapers, magazines, and television stations clamoured to interview her. She loved every moment of it. Soon she assumed all the airs and graces of a celebrity. She would no longer eat around the corner at Steverino's Grill with station staff. She was inundated with invitations to dinner in elegant restaurants, galas, balls, and nightclubs.

Gordon hadn't set eyes on her for the past month. She was never home when he called. And he couldn't get through to her while she was at the station as the switchboard was always jammed. Even when the line was free she was either at a meeting or an interview. He left messages at first but she never returned his calls.

She did think of him from time to time, but only in the most fleeting way. He had become a shadow of the past in her mind and his memory was blurred out by the fast-moving merry-go-round in which she now spun. She wanted nothing to do with her past, and that's where Gordon belonged.

Ah what the heck, Gordon thought to himself twirling a pencil, if she needs me, she knows where to find me. It was clear she didn't need him and this caused him the sharpest feeling of hurt and disappointment. Not so long ago she couldn't live without him, and he had actually discouraged the physical relationship that she so ardently desired. He cursed that cautionary voice inside him that told him to steer clear until she got herself together. She was very together now and he was very left behind. He smiled ruefully. Anyway he never seemed to have luck when it came to women. At least it was only him getting hurt this time. He looked at his watch, time for lunch, and he left his desk and went out to his car.

He'd had the old Ford for a long time. Maybe if he got a Jaguar Margaret Anne would notice him. He'd always secretly yearned for a Jaguar. Don't be stupid, he told himself, it's not the car, it's the man. He pulled down the mirror and looked at his reflection. He was handsome enough, and Mags had once thought he was the greatest.

Oh hell, he said to himself, suddenly overcome by an urgent desire to see her. I"ll do it, he thought, and drove off in the direction of Gold FM. She would be off the air in a little over half an hour. He tuned into her show and the warmth of her voice flowed through his entire being. He parked and listened until the end of her shift.

A few minutes later he saw her leave the building and, as he walked across the sidewalk to greet her, it struck him how truly beautiful she was with her blonde hair bouncing around her flawless face with its huge, vivid, blue eyes.

"Hi, Mags," he exclaimed breathlessly as they met face to face. "I was getting anxious about you," he stammered on, his words coming out in a rush.

"I felt you were giving me the cold shoulder or something like that."

Margaret Anne blushed slightly and then lifted her face to his. He kissed her affectionately and, squeezing her hand tightly, asked, "Can you spare even one night in the week to meet an old friend? I've been missing you lately."

He noticed her lips begin to quiver and he detected that old stubborn look in her eyes.

"Gordon, I'm sorry, I just have no social life. I haven't a minute, honest, I haven't. I barely get time to sleep."

"Why? The job is surely not that demanding. What are you up to? You're not ... "

She was indignant now. How could he suspect her of weakly lapsing back into her old ways?

"I most certainly am not doing any drugs, if that's what you're asking. What I am doing, and surely you ought to know, is trying to keep my public happy. I have to be all things to all people, and honey, that's a full-time job."

He was about to speak, but she cut him off.

"I've got to go Gordon, I have a luncheon and I'm late already. See you around, take care."

She called this last part out to him as she disappeared into the parking lot. She was gone. A little, rueful smile tinged his lips as he said to himself ah well, life's a bitch. Just when he had begun to see Margaret Anne through new eyes, the eyes of love. She was perfect for him in every way. She was the woman he needed --strong, intelligent, charming, outgoing. And such perfect poise and manner. If only she had the time for him.

Meanwhile, Margaret Anne had scurried deep into the parking lot and was about to open the door of her new, white Fiat when she was caught from behind. Both of her hands were yanked roughly behind her back. She jerked her neck to glimpse a tall man in a black ski-mask. Before she could scream a strong, gloved hand clamped over her mouth. She struggled and kicked fiercely but her assailant was far stronger and bundled her roughly into the back seat of the grey car parked beside hers. She felt a sharp knee dig into her back as a white scarf was tied roughly in her mouth. She tried to bite the gloved fingers, but the scarf was tightened and her cries and screams were muffled. In a matter of seconds her arms and feet were also bound.

The knee lifted and she was pushed onto the car's floor. She heard two doors slam and then the engine hum to life. She tried to squirm and wriggle her way to the seat as the car began to pull away. What was going on? All she knew at that moment was that she was trapped in a car with a mad man who seemed to have some sort of vendetta against her. She was scared almost to death. She kicked the back of his seat frantically, gritting her teeth in anger. At last she wriggled up to the seat. There was a darkened pane of glass between her and the driver. She writhed and put her face to the window to see if she could attract someone's attention. Cars, vans and trucks thundered along at each side of the car, but no one took any notice of her. Nobody took much notice of anything in San Diego. Her fury and frustration mounted and she let out muffled shrieks and moans of anger and indignation, though she knew they were useless. Suddenly she felt her ankles shift. Her writhing had loosened the cord that bound them. She slowly, patiently tried to loosen them further.

They had travelled about fifty miles when the car turned off the freeway and some five minutes later came to a halt outside a large, black timber gate. The driver got out to open it. She glanced at his back and imagined there was something familiar about him. But she spared no time for that. She had her feet loose and kneeling on the seat she leaned forward and opened the lock with her teeth. She then loosened the door handle in the same way, quietly pushed the door open with the top of her head, and twisted to get her feet on the ground. She then sprang up, ready to run. But there he was, laughing. His mask was off. It was Tyrone.

He grabbed her by the hair as he had once before, took her through the gate and walked her past several parked cars to a dingy, grey caravan. Tears streamed down her face as he opened the door and pushed her inside.

The heavy, floral drapes were drawn and it took some time for her eyes to adjust to the scene within. She gasped and almost fainted at the sight which confronted her. There, on the long, brown-and-beige plaid sofa sat Jonathan Khan with her son Bikram on his knee. Jonathan was dressed in a blue and white t-shirt with spotless white slacks, and he smiled in the most chilling way.

Bikram cooed and for some reason this calmed her. She sensed she wasn't going to be hurt. Jonathan was a cool, reasonable man. She looked at the baby. He was a picture, wearing just blue linen short pants over his bronze legs.

"How's everything for you, Marianna?" Jonathan asked. "I hear you are quite a celebrity now."

Margaret Anne said nothing, and Jonathan looked lovingly at the baby.

"Aren't you proud of your beautiful Mum?" he asked it.

Margaret Anne still couldn't find words and just stood there like someone in a daze.

"Untie her and make her comfortable, Tyrone."

"Yes sir."

Tyrone leered as he undid the bonds. She looked at him with disdain in her icy eyes and now it was not fear, but a boiling wave of temper, which prevented her from uttering a syllable. Jonathan stood up, came towards her, and took her gently by the hand. His fingers were cool and gentle and despite herself she let him lead her to the sofa where she sat down feeling completely mystified.

"You don't appear to have much to say for a lady who makes her living with her voice, Marianna," Jonathan remarked in a soft, polite tone of voice.

"I guess Mags O'Dowd don't talk now without her mike," Tyrone said, throwing back his head and laughing bitterly.

Her eyes were flashing now and she couldn't contain her anger a moment longer.

"I wouldn't talk to scum like you with or without a microphone."

She then fixed her angry gaze on Jonathan.

"Isn't it about time you told me what I am doing in this place and why I was abducted on my way to a very urgent meeting? From which my absence will be noted, I might add. What the hell is going on here?"

Jonathan remained totally unruffled and his lips held a smug, cynical smile "Take it easy now, Marianna, you're getting all uptight. Don't let old Tyrone upset you so. He doesn't mean anything. He's just a joker, that's all."

"I'm not the slightest bit interested in that animal. I want answers to my questions and I want them now."

"You disappoint me, Marianna," he said mockingly. "I thought you would be happy to spend some time with your son."

He reached down and lifted a smiling Bikram up to her.

"He's adorable isn't he? Come take him in your arms and cuddle him. He loves to be hugged."

Before she had a chance to refuse, the baby was in her arms and two quick flashes blinded her. The screaming baby was taken from her and bursts of colour exploded before her eyes. When they finally adjusted, they saw Tyrone removing a photograph from an instamatic camera. She suddenly realised what was happening. She stood up and ran towards the door. But Jonathan was standing with his back to it.

"Too late, my sweet. We have what we want and we intend to use it if we do not receive your full cooperation."

She was stunned now and she could feel the blood drain from her face. She felt completely rooted to the spot, but she managed to ask, "What do you want of me?"

"It's really a matter of pride," Jonathan said, beckoning to Tyrone, who handed him the photographs.

Jonathan studied them closely and then, holding them up for Margaret Anne to see, said, "Isn't that just beautiful, mother and son, how lovely. Of course the paper would have proof from me anyway, but these pictures will add so much to the story. Mags O'Dowd and the fifteen-month-old son she sold for ten thousand dollars. What would your beloved listeners think of that? I dare say your popularity would drop drastically. You couldn't possibly allow that to happen, could you?"

Margaret Anne was appalled. "Why?" she asked.

"Because of you, my son started out life with a price tag over his head. A badge of shame. I can not be easy until that is removed. This baby is priceless. And he is growing up where he belongs. He is mine, not because I paid for him, but because that's how it was meant to be. You will give me back that ten thousand dollars and remove the shame from his head."

A crazy, evil gleam shone in his eyes. This guy was crazy, she suddenly realised. The cool exterior was only a guise. He might do anything.

In a steady, controlled voice, she replied, "I guess you have me where you want me, so I don't have much choice but to do as you ask. Otherwise my career is down the tubes."

"Smart bitch," Tyrone quipped, but she ignored him and kept her eyes rivetted on Jonathan.

He went to his briefcase, opened it up, and took out a small portable telephone.

"Take this," he began, "ring your bank and tell them to prepare the bank draft for ten thousand payable to me. You and I will go and collect it, and then you will have no more hassle from me."

"But I haven't any money in the bank," she replied, trembling now. "Believe me I haven't a dime."

He looked curiously and enquiringly at her.

"You certainly know how to get rid of money quickly," he remarked and she knew that he did not believe her.

"Come with me to my bank. I'll get a statement of my account. You'll see that I'm borrowed up to the hilt. I've just bought a car."

"We could always take the car," Tyrone interjected.

"Oh no, Tyrone. Of course our Marianna will be able to raise that paltry sum, she being such a big name now."

"But where will I raise it? I don't have a clue who to go to."

He handed her the telephone.

"Here take this, and think of somebody, quick."

What was she going to do now? She tried to think clearly and make some kind of sense out of this mess. She had to find the money, of that she was absolutely certain, but where? Her boss? No, she eliminated Ron Harte straight away. He was a shrewd man and if she asked him for that kind of money, in a hurry, he would guess that there was something amiss, no matter what yarn she spun. Gordon? Nine months ago definitely, but after the terrible way she'd treated him lately, would he? Anyway Ron and himself were great friends and he might even be tempted to confide in him. No, that would be too dangerous. She was left with the one remaining option, her parents. And when the chips were down she guessed they were the only ones she could really trust. She took the telephone in her hand and dialled the number.

CHAPTER 8

The afternoon had grown oppressively hot and sultry. Gráinne came in from the garden to the welcome coolness of the lounge. She poured herself a cup of iced tea and sat on the rocking chair with her feet up on the plush, pink footstool. The telephone's ringing seemed exceptionally loud in the still tranquillity of the house, and it startled her slightly. She jumped up, lifted the receiver swiftly, and breathlessly said hello.

"Hi Mum, it's me."

Margaret Anne was under the sharp scrutiny of Jonathan Khan, who had warned her not to give any information either about the purpose for which she required the cash or of her present whereabouts.

"Hello Margaret Anne. I was just sitting here thinking about you and that wonderful lady you interviewed this morning."

It was strange and somewhat soothing to hear her mother's friendly, familiar voice talking about ordinary things. But she could not forget for long the hostile environment she had found herself in.

"Is Dad home?" she asked hopefully, ignoring her mother's remarks.

"No, sure you know he's never here at this hour of the day. Is there something wrong?"

"Not really, Mum. It's just that I need a pretty large sum of money rather urgently. Right now, in fact."

Gráinne was disturbed now. She caught something odd in her daughter's voice, a nuance that worried her. Had she lapsed into her old ways again? Many were the drunken calls she'd received in days gone by pleading for money. But no, she didn't sound like that at all. This was different somehow.

"Where are you?" Gráinne asked, trembling slightly now.

Margaret Anne hesitated, covering the mouthpiece to consult with Jonathan.

"You may give her this number," he said, jotting it down on a piece of paper.

"Don't ask any questions right now, Mum. Try to contact Dad and tell him to ring me right away at this number."

Gráinne reached for a pen and notepad and hastily scribbled down the number her daughter read out.

"Remember, it's very urgent, and I'm depending on you."

The phone clicked off, leaving Gráinne in a state of extreme fear and anxiety. The tension in Margaret Anne's voice had been unmistakable. There was no doubt in her mind that Margaret Anne was in some sort of trouble. The sooner she got in touch with Eoin, the better. For her own sake as well as for Margaret Anne's. Gráinne always fell to pieces in a crisis, but Eoin was strong. He would handle the situation, whatever it was.

Meanwhile, in the caravan, Margaret Anne was now alone with Jonathan. He had ordered Tyrone to take the baby away, his purpose having been served. All that remained for them to do was to wait until Eoin made contact.

"My father won't be able to get this cash today. The banks are closed and he doesn't keep that kind of money in the house."

"I'm not in any great hurry. I have all the time in the world. But I presume you would like to be at your post in time for your programme tomorrow."

"You mean you will hold me here until you actually get the cash?" Margaret Anne asked almost hysterically.

"But of course," he answered as he reached for a cigar and began to light it.

"That doesn't make any sense," Margaret Anne said, almost in tears now. "You know I have to come up with the goods or face the consequences."

"Oh, but my pretty one, there are many things you could do. I am a man of the world, you see, and I know all the tricks. I'm not prepared to take any chances. Anyway, you will be quite comfortable here. It's a pleasant little van and the air conditioning is quite effective, isn't it?"

He was so cool, so suave, so utterly tantalizing that she wanted to kill him.

The phone rang. She glanced at Jonathan who nodded. She jumped up and answered it on the third ring.

"Is that you, Dad?" she asked almost breathlessly.

"Yes, it's me. What's this all about? Your mother is at her wit's end. Why did you have to upset her?"

Margaret Anne threw her eyes up to heaven. Her mother again, that's all he cares about.

"But Dad, I'm frantic. I'm in a big mess, and I need ten thousand dollars immediately."

"Ten thousand dollars?" he gasped. "Where do you think I could get that kind of money? And why so quickly and so suddenly?"

"I can't give you any more information now. But try to understand that it's vital that I get it. My reputation and my job are on the line."

Despite her best efforts she was crying bitterly now.

"Come home, and we'll discuss it, and we'll see what can be done."

"I can't, I can't, don't you see I have to stay here until I get the cash? Oh please, Dad, help me. I need it now."

Eoin was flabbergasted. He could hardly believe his ears, and for once in his life he didn't know what to do. She sounded so frantic, and for the life of him he couldn't understand what was going on.

"Is this a ransom? Have you been kidnapped? For God's sake, Margaret Anne, pull yourself together and tell me what, exactly, the story is."

"No it's not like that at all, but I can't, you see. I can't tell you any more. Just get the money somewhere and I'll pay it back."

"Why can't you make some repayment plan? I'll personally guarantee the money."

"That's no good. Believe me I would if I could, but it's just not possible."

This wasn't making any kind of sense to Eoin. Exasperated now, tired of Margaret Anne's escapades, he said, "Listen here, Margaret Anne, I have been bailing you out of nasty situations for a long time now and I can not continue to do so any longer. I have a sizeable bank overdraft and a lot of bills to be paid, and I think it's high time you were able to stand on your own two feet and get yourself out of this one the way you got yourself into it."

The line was dead. She couldn't believe it. She held the receiver in her hand and looked at it in absolute horror and dismay.

"He hung up, he actually hung up on me," she repeated over and over again.

"Too bad my dear," she heard Jonathan Khan's soft smug voice intone. She turned to face him, her face white as a lily, her big, blue eyes ablaze with anger.

"You bastard, you shit-eating coloured pig. I hate you. I hate you, and I'll get back at you some day, believe me, I will."

"You have nothing to say about me, Miss O'Dowd. I can get ten thousand dollars, if not more, quite legally and legitimately from a certain newspaper for this story. I was merely being concerned and considerate and giving you a chance to save yourself. I'm so sorry it didn't work out that way, but there is nothing more I can do. As soon as Tyrone returns he will take you back home."

"Couldn't you let me pay you off weekly?" she pleaded.

"Sorry, sweetest. No deal."

CHAPTER 9

Margaret Anne did not return home that night. Desperately needing to be alone with her thoughts, she stayed in the Day's Inn Motel beside the harbour in Tulavista where it was quiet and peaceful. She walked down to the marina in the late afternoon breeze and stood on the pier, watching the yachts with their multi-coloured sails as they swayed gently on the calm, rippling water. She caught sight of the Mermaid docked there, as large and luxurious as ever. She'd spent many wild nights on board with Nicky. She toyed with the idea of paying him a visit. A few drinks and a snort of coke would wipe away all her fears. But some mysterious inner being seemed to be warning her to steer clear. And, in spite of herself, she did just that.

Back in the motel, as she lay in the hot, soothing bubble bath, allowing her body to relax, her life stood out before her as though on a movie screen. It had been a crazy, turbulent life for certain. And just when it had settled down at last to some sort of even keel, it was again set to toss wildly in the wind.

She badly wanted to talk to Gordon. She felt he might be able to help, but pride would not allow her to ring him. She was still angry with her father, but on further reflection she had to admit that he was in a very difficult situation, not knowing the full facts. He'll soon know everything, she thought to herself and she cringed at the prospect of what lay ahead. She knew that hearing how she'd sold the baby would deeply disturb both her parents. They had assumed that she had the best interests of the child at heart but now they would know the ugly truth. She'd sold her baby. Oh, how could she have done such a thing? These genuine pangs of regret amazed her. What was happening to the old, hard Margaret Anne O'Dowd? She could still see her baby's beautiful little face with the big, innocent, brown eyes and she was struck with deep remorse at how the little creature had been used by everyone. But there was no point in recriminations now. He was well and truly signed out of her life, and there was nothing she could do about it. Nor was there anything she could do to stop the story coming out. She forced herself to laugh under her breath in an effort to shake off the fear of what loomed ahead. But it came out small, frightened, and timid.

She was on air as usual at eleven the next morning. A true professional, she left her worries outside the studio door. The show, as always, was delivered in her trademark, bright and entertaining style. She interviewed her guests, spun her discs, interspersing cheery and witty comments throughout.

In Chula Vista, Gráinne was immensely relieved to hear her daughter's voice through her radio since she hadn't heard from her since yesterday's phone call. While Gráinne listened to the interview, Eoin rang home from work. He too was overjoyed at the fact that she was free and well. There'd been a message from her for him at work saying she was fine and that she was staying on her own at a motel for a few days to gather her thoughts.

"Oh, thank God. I made the right decision after all," he sighed to Gráinne through the phone lines.

"And do you see how she found her own solution to her own problem? We've been pampering her all along."

"You were right, Eoin. Thank God things worked out for her."

Five days later, just when Margaret Anne was beginning to lapse into a feeling of some security, the story broke. In homes across the area, people woke to the screaming, bold headline

"RADIO CELEBRITY MAGS O'DOWD SOLD HER SON".

Beneath the large, black letters was set the picture of Margaret Anne in the caravan, holding Bikram, a startled look on both their faces.

Thankfully, she had taken refuge in her quiet motel and no one knew where to find her. She was blissfully unaware of the very unpleasant scenes taking place at her home since early that morning. Reporters and television camera men swarmed like ants all around the outside of the house. The telephone rang without pause until Eoin finally took it off the hook. Gráinne wandered about the house, knocking against walls and furniture, wailing. Eoin was at his wit's end trying to cope with her hysterical ravings. He'd done his utmost to calm her but to no avail. She continued to cry aloud and to wander, pale and disoriented.

"Get these people away. We're ruined, oh God, we're ruined. We'll never live this down. Take me home to Ireland. I won't stay here a moment longer. I hate this, this godforsaken country. We haven't had a minute's peace since we set foot here," she sobbed.

"Take it easy now, love," Eoin said, trying to guide her to the sofa. "This will pass. You know these things are only a nine days wonder. Soon everything will be back to normal."

But she wasn't listening to a word he said. She ranted on and on, screaming loudly. Her sobs and screams even drowned out the vociferous men and women outside, who banged doors and windows in their efforts to gain access. Eoin began to fear his wife might lapse into insanity. The shock of the news combined with the strain of all this media pestering might be so great that it would seriously unbalance her highly strung personality. He poured her a stiff brandy and said, "Here, drink this. It will help you."

"Nothing will help me anymore. I've had it, Eoin. This is the end. I want to die."

Eoin reached out to comfort her, but she shook his hand away.

"For God's sake just leave me alone!" she screamed and ran upstairs like someone completely demented.

She locked herself into the bathroom, where he could still hear her sobbing wildly. I can not allow this to continue, he thought, shaking now himself. She might do herself some injury. He reached for the telephone and called the police, angrily explaining his predicament. He was grateful for their concern and understanding, and extremely relieved a short time later when a squad car arrived and dispersed the crowd of vultures. He should have thought of telling the police they were disturbing their peace and tormenting his wife long ago, but things were happening so quickly that his own mind wasn't functioning normally. And these days he was always so weak. His daughter had certainly shaken things up again.

Margaret Anne sat by the window of her room and stared blankly out at the Asia-blue sky, cursing Jonathan Khan and his vile accomplice Tyrone. Why was this happening to her just when she had started to achieve some status in her own right, from her own hard work? For the past months she'd been living her life just as she liked it, with the maximum of pleasure and attention from others. She did not miss the drugs at all. But now she squirmed at the gloomy prospect of her future. Ron Harte had been interviewed by a leading television reporter earlier. He'd said unequivocally that he was disgusted, bitterly disappointed, and definitely never aware of any improprieties on her part. He said he had been charmed and fooled like all the rest of us. He went on to assure the man that he couldn't see the day that would bring Mags O'Dowd back to the air waves. She'd switched off the set after that statement. She wouldn't bother even to call him now. He had made his position patently obvious. Now she was a nobody again. She brought her fist down on the motel bed and gritted her teeth. She could not be a nobody. This was totally contrary to her idea of how life should be lived. She needed power, money, and celebrity. But now she couldn't even leave this small room. If she went outside the door she could be lynched, so bitter was public opinion against her right now. How fickle the public are, she thought to herself. A few hours ago they adored me, and now they're out for my blood.

She walked across the room and looked at her reflection in the mirror. She looked tired and weak. She ran her fingers through her hair. Goodbye, Mags O'Dowd, she said to herself with a bitter little laugh. You were great and powerful, but now you're dead. If you're lucky you'll be allowed to return to your good, righteous, God-fearing parents. Your father will be loud in his condemnations of you and how you caused your poor mother so much hurt and pain. He won't understand your own human frailty and he won't be concerned that your life has caved in around you just when you were making great headway. He won't understand the supreme effort you made to kick the habit and how tough that was, and of course he won't consider the heartbreak you yourself are suffering. She broke down at that point, threw herself on the bed, and cried until she had no more tears to shed. She badly needed a drink but she couldn't even go across the grounds to the bar for fear of being recognised. There was only one person in the whole world who could help her now as always. Throwing her pride to the wind, she dialled his office number.

"Star Enterprises, may I help you?"

"Gordon Edwards, please," she requested quietly.

"Can I say who is speaking, ma'am?"

"It's personal," she replied in a cold, tense voice.

"All right, ma'am, hold on please."

As she waited Margaret Anne found herself actually praying that he would be there. She couldn't stand being alone in this place one moment longer.

"Gordon Edwards here."

"Hi Gordon. It's me, Mags."

"Oh God, Mags, I've been worried out of my mind. I've searched everywhere for you. Are you okay? Where are you?"

"I'm at the Day's Inn in Tulavista. Can you come?"

"I'll be over right away. Hang in there, kid."

She replaced the receiver and felt nearly lightheaded from a strong surge from within herself -- a mixture of blissful relief combined with the strong affection she'd been repressing for months for this man who was always there for her in spite of everything. As the minutes ticked by she could not believe how anxious she was for Gordon to come, how much she looked forward to seeing him, to being with him. She didn't have to put on a front with Gordon. She could just be herself, and that was exactly how he wanted her. She wished he would not only come over and comfort her but take her away, far away from this place. To a place where they could really be together for a while, alone. She went into the bathroom and brushed her hair. Her eyes were red and a bit swollen, so she quickly dabbed on some make-up and then lit the last cigarette she had left.

Taking her third of fourth puff, she heard footsteps on the little narrow concrete path outside the window. Then the bell rang. Her heart racing, she glanced through the window just to be quite sure. Then she opened the door. He took her in his strong arms and she didn't resist and they remained in silence holding each other for several moments. Then he took her face in both his hands, and gently lifting it up towards his, he kissed her lightly on the cheek. Then, removing a strand of blonde hair which hung over her eyes, he kissed her again. She looked up at him with her huge, tear-filled eyes and he couldn't help thinking how lost and defenceless she was.

"Don't worry, Mags," he said. "It's not as bad as it seems. You'll find another way to make it, I know you will. Sweetheart, you've got what it takes. Haven't you proved that already? I'm proud of you, lady."

"Oh Gordon," she cried, "don't you see? I've had it. I'm really finished now. I'll never be anyone again."

"Once a star, always a star, Mags. And you know what they say --any publicity is good publicity."

She couldn't stand to hear the cliché, especially when in her case it was so patently false. This publicity was disastrous, it was as simple as that. "Be serious, Gordon," she said, slightly irritated. "What am I going to do?"

"Let it all cool down for a while," he replied thoughtfully. "And we'll see what happens. Things might not be as bad as you think. Tell you what, let's go away for a while, a week or two, just you and I. You know what they say -- when the going gets tough, the tough get going."

She laughed at that, and yes, she liked the idea. Hadn't she just been wishing for it moments before? It appealed to her except for one thing. Was he making some hasty presumptions?

"No strings attached?" she asked with a wry smile.

"Whatever and wherever pleases you," he grinned back at her.

What a fabulous guy he is, she thought. If only he were rich and famous. She knew herself too well. She couldn't get by without power and money.

"A penny for your thoughts," he said.

That's the problem, I'll need someone who's able to pay a lot more than that, she thought sadly to herself.

"Oh, they're not worth it," is what she said aloud. "I was just thinking where we could go."

"Let's decide over dinner," he said, putting his hand in his jacket pocket. He withdrew a pair of black sunglasses. "Here, wear these just in case."

Margaret Anne smiled.

"Thanks, Gordon. You think of everything, don't you?"

"Only things that concern a certain person," he said, winking mischievously.

CHAPTER 10

It was a stifling, early Spring evening and Eoin languished on the couch, looking strange and wooden. Gráinne sat beside him, lost in a light sleep. The air-conditioner was broken and the room felt heavy and still. It had been almost two weeks now since Eoin had been to work, and it had taken him all of that time to bring his wife round to some semblance of normality.

Until just a few days ago he would still find one or two persistent reporters sniffing around the place until he chased them off. He sighed and sank deeper into the couch. It had been a glorious day, but now dusk was falling. And he had a very early start in the morning. He looked at Gráinne as she dozed peacefully beside him. He placed a hand on his sleeping wife's shoulder. Gráinne had been happy today after speaking to Margaret Anne on the phone. And although Margaret Anne wouldn't say where she was, Gráinne wasn't worried because Gordon was with her.

"There is something very sincere and genuine about that lad," she had said. "He's a rock of sense and he is very good for Margaret Anne."

As Eoin stared at her he began to shiver, filling with melancholy and feeling unexpectedly sad. It worried him that she was so totally dependent on him, that she had no other interests or friends outside of him. She was very highly strung and always went to pieces over the smallest problem. His mind rambled back to that evening several months ago. As always, he was almost stunned by the memory. He could see it all so clearly: Dr Matthew Josephs sitting behind his desk, taking off his glasses, looking him straight in the eye. Dr Josephs' countenance had conveyed the grim message before he had spoken a word.

"I'm afraid, Eoin, that the prognosis is not good. Let me give it to you straight," he'd said, standing up, pinning the x-ray onto the little screen behind him.

"Do you see this dark area here around the liver? Well, this is where the cancer is located, and I'm afraid it's inoperable. I'm sorry, Eoin, but that's how it is."

Eoin remembered that numbed, dazed feeling, followed by the anger, and then the heartbreak. He cried like a baby before asking the next question.

"How much time have I got, Doctor?"

"With medication and a bit of luck, a year. Maybe a little more or less, it's difficult to say with absolute certainty."

But, sitting restless on the couch, it was not for himself that Eoin felt uneasy. He had resigned himself to his fate some time ago. No, it was Gráinne he was worried about. What would become of her? He had made all the necessary financial arrangements for her, and in that regard she would be very comfortable. But he felt instinctively that she would pine away without him. He'd racked his brains to find a solution, but of course there was no way he could tell her. He sat up straight and pulled himself together, not daring to allow these feelings to get a grip on him. He had to be strong for her, at least while he was still here with her. The grim reality of it sent shivers through his body.

In normal circumstances a man's daughter should be a source of consolation to him, he thought. He should be feeling some degree of peace, knowing that she would be a comfort to her mother. But unfortunately the opposite appeared to be true, a fact that he strongly resented. He thought of Margaret Anne, now hiding somewhere from the grievous scandal that had been so widely publicised, a scandal that had brought such great pain and shame on her poor mother. He wished with all his heart that he could forget about the whole affair, and just let happen what would happen. But of course that would be totally selfish of him. And, anyway, he didn't want to die and be buried in this country. He would have to sell this house and return to Ireland. He'd have to put the wheels in motion very soon now. But how to explain this decision was the problem. He looked up at the picture of the Sacred Heart and he whispered a little prayer for the courage and strength to make the correct decision and to keep going for as long as it took. If only he could tell Margaret Anne, talk to her heart to heart, father to daughter, and discuss his plans with her. If only he could rely on her to take care of her mother after he was gone, he wouldn't feel so very worried. He'd considered telling her but he was afraid of what her reaction would be. She might easily go off the deep end herself and start to take those terrible drugs again. It might be as good an excuse as any for her. Besides, the poor girl had enough on her plate just now. In her present circumstances anyway, it was out of the question. So he had no other choice but to bear the heavy burden all on his own. He got up to make himself a hot drink, and, as he did so, the telephone rang loud and shrill in the stillness of the house.

Gráinne jumped up with a start, her eyes immediately clenching back shut against the light of the lamp.

"Who is it? What time is it?" she asked sleepily, as Eoin picked up the receiver.

"Hello, Gordon," she heard her husband say and she immediately pricked up her ears.

"Eoin, I'm ringing from a hospital in San Francisco," Gordon continued. "Margaret Anne is in Theatre. She's broken her jaw bone. There was an accident in a department store. She fell down an escalator."

"Oh God, is she all right?" he whispered into the receiver.

"She'll be fine, there's nothing to worry about. They're wiring the jaw together so it will heal."

Eoin watched his words, conscious of Gráinne's presence beside him.

"I'm sorry to hear that Gordon, but it could be a lot worse."

"Yes, I suppose in a sense she's lucky. It will be painful but she'll be okay. She'll probably need to have a bit of reconstructive surgery later."

"Oh?"

"Nothing major. And guess what? Standing beside me here I have the plastic surgeon himself. And you'll never guess who it is."

"Neil!" Eoin said immediately.

Of course, Gordon had said they were in San Francisco, hadn't he? And Neil O'Grady, the son of Gráinne's sister, Deirdre, was the top plastic surgeon there.

"Right you are, Eoin. I'll put him on to you now."

Gráinne was leaning nervously against Eoin and slightly alarmed at this stage.

"What's wrong, Eoin?"

"Nothing serious," he whispered. "Go up to the extension in the bedroom and you'll hear everything first hand."

"How are you, Eoin?"

"Neil, what's going on?" Gráinne asked breathlessly.

"Oh hi, Gráinne." Neil's voice was cheerful and reassuring as he described Margaret Anne's condition.

"So she'll be as good as new in no time," he finished.

"Is she in pain?" Gráinne whispered.

"To a certain extent, but she'll get plenty of medication for that. She will, of course, have to be fed through a straw and won't be able to speak until her jaw heals."

"But that's terrible," Gráinne said.

"My poor child. Nothing seems to go right for her. And will her face be ..."

Gráinne couldn't finish the question.

"Not at all," Neil said reassuringly.

"With a little bit of surgery she'll look exactly as she did before. She had her accident in the right place, anyway. California is the world's capital of plastic surgery."

"And who better to do the job than her own first cousin?" Eoin said cheerfully.

"Exactly. I'll make sure she retains the family's good looks."

"When can we see her?" Eoin asked.

"Better leave it for a while. I'll be in touch with you again in a few days. In the meantime there's no need to worry. She's in good hands."

Soon after the call Eoin and Gráinne went to bed. Eoin lay awake for a long time that night. Neil would be the ideal person to talk to about his own predicament. And his advice would be sound. Why hadn't he thought of it before? Probably the fact that he was Gráinne's nephew and when he rang he usually spoke more to Gráinne than to him had something to do with it. Not to mention the fact that his mind was so addled with all the worry over Gráinne that he'd overlooked nearly everything else. He would ring Neil from the office tomorrow and arrange to meet him. Funny, he thought, how Margaret Anne's accident had brought a possible answer to his prayer.

CHAPTER 11

Neil immediately detected the strong sense of urgency in Eoin's voice. His uncle refused to give any clue to the nature of his problem except that it definitely had no bearing upon Margaret Anne. Eoin said it would be difficult for him to get to San Francisco because he did not, under any circumstances, want Gráinne to find out about any of this, but that he would try to take a day off during the week. Neil silenced Eoin 's objections and said he would fly to San Diego to meet him on the following Sunday, his day off. They would meet at a hotel near Eoin's home. Eoin again stressed the necessity of keeping their meeting a secret from Gráinne. Neil hung up the phone worried, and he remained so until he met Eoin that Sunday.

Eoin was tense and held himself rigidly as he sat on the very large, red, leather armchair in the hotel's lobby. Neil sat opposite him and tried to appear cheerful, making small talk while he himself also felt anxious and apprehensive. In spite of his problems, Eoin couldn't help noticing how elegant Neil looked in his perfectly-tailored white suit with navy shirt and tie. He had certainly changed a lot from the gangly Irish lad from Glenbeg who had visited Gráinne and himself more than ten years ago. Eoin took the glass of whiskey from the table in front of him and swallowed it back in one gulp. Then, taking a deep breath and summoning his courage, he began.

"There is no point in beating around the bush, Neil. You're a doctor yourself and you probably are quite accustomed to this line. I'm dying, Neil -- cancer of the liver. I have about twelve months."

It was Neil's turn to take a large sip of his drink now. He was stunned. A surge of overwhelming pity for his uncle would not allow him to speak. It took him several seconds to come to terms with this devastating news. He felt helpless and inadequate. This was the man who had taken him into his home many years ago when Neil was just a boy. That trip to Eoin and Gráinne had been one of the best experiences of his life. He had loved California ever since and had always felt very close to both of them. But what could he do or say that would be of the slightest assistance to him now? Words were like straw blowing in the wind on occasions like this.

"I'm so terribly sorry, Eoin," he tried to say but the words strangled in his throat.

"I know that, Neil, but sure, that's life, isn't it?"

Neil steadied himself now and managed somehow to regain his self-possession.

"Are you absolutely sure that nothing can be done, no treatment or surgery? Great advances have been made in the treatment of cancer today."

"No, I've gone into every possible aspect of it, and, without giving you the sordid details, all I can tell you is that in my case the growths are inoperable. I'm receiving some treatment that may arrest its progress but, having said that, I still have only a year. All the tests and biopsies are quite conclusive."

"How are you feeling now?" Neil asked, noticing the slightly jaundiced colour around Eoin's neck.

"The pain can be pretty awful at times. But so far anyway the tablets do the trick. I believe that won't be so in a month or two. And that's what I want to talk to you about."

Neil was alert now.

"If there is anything in this world I can do for you, Eoin, you can count absolutely on me."

"I know that, and thanks a lot."

Then, puckering his eyebrows for a moment, Eoin resumed: "my main worry is Gráinne. You know how she is. And I find it impossible to tell her. Margaret Anne isn't much better, mind you. In fact, maybe she's worse. And that's my main dilemma. You see, Neil, I need to sell out and return to Ireland. And I just don't know how to begin, what explanation I should give, and how I'm going to cope with all the legalities."

Eoin's voice grew faint at that stage and Neil could see that he was holding back tears. It was a very difficult situation, of that there was no doubt. Nevertheless, it must be tackled immediately. Time was of the essence.

"Don't upset yourself about it. We're in this together now and we'll get moving right away. Margaret Anne must be told immediately. And what better time to tell her than now when she's in hospital? She's safe there, and I'll be with her all the time. What do you think?"

"Yes, I think you're right. I suppose I should tell her myself. I've never had a really close relationship with her. It will be quite hard."

"It must come from you, Eoin. But if you want me to be there then I certainly will."

"I'd appreciate that very much. When can I see her?"

"Let's say two weeks from today. Gráinne and yourself can visit her, and I'll make sure that you and I get time alone with her. That's settled, then?"

Eoin agreed and Neil could see that he was relieved already.

"I presume you have all your affairs in order," Neil added. "I mean, you have a will made."

"I haven't done that as yet, but I will in the next few days. That's something else. I shouldn't ask, Neil, but would you act as my executor?"

"Certainly, my privilege. And you know you can rest assured that everything will be carried out just as you wish."

"I'm know that, Neil. I'm most grateful."

"Think nothing of it. That's what family is for."

Then Neil had a sudden thought.

"You know, Eoin," he continued, "if you want to go home as soon as possible, I could arrange the sale of the house in your absence. That could be mentioned in your will in case the sale hadn't been completed before, before ..."

"Yes," Eoin interjected.

"I think that's an excellent idea. I just hope it all works out."

"We'll see that it does. Gráinne will be delighted to go home, I would imagine. And, who knows, maybe Margaret Anne will feel the same if it's your dying wish and everything."

"I wish we were home right now. I feel so frightened and insecure here."

"I can understand that. But hang in there. It won't be long now, I promise you."

CHAPTER 12

"Maybe you can try to speak today," Neil suggested to Margaret Anne as he stood beside her bed with Gordon. Yesterday the wires had been removed, but she'd been too scared to talk.

"Neil," she murmured without moving her lips and in the smallest of voices.

"That's my girl," Neil said.

Gordon bent down to kiss her.

"I also have a lovely surprise for you," Neil announced.

"You have?" came the small, little voice again.

"Your mum and dad are coming to see you today. They should be here in about an hour, so sit up there and do yourself up. We want you to look your best."

She was smiling a tight, little smile now and pointing to the locker beside her bed. Gordon knew exactly what she wanted and took out her cosmetic bag and handed it to her.

Neil's smile twitched slightly. What would she do when she saw her face in the mirror? The last thing he needed now was a tantrum.

"Now, your face may not be as perfect as it was, Margaret Anne," he said, raising a cautionary finger, "but we'll do a little bit of plastic surgery as soon as possible and it will be as beautiful as ever."

Margaret Anne had the small compact mirror out. She shut her eyes, breathed deeply, then opened them and looked at herself. It was not nearly as bad as she'd feared, just a small sharpness to her jawline.

"It's not too bad," she said faintly, examining it closely.

"I can't see a thing wrong with it," Gordon remarked. "It would be difficult to ruin that gorgeous profile."

Neil breathed a sigh of relief. Thank God for that, he said to himself. He just hoped the next hurdle would be as easily overcome.

Gordon, sitting on the bed with his arm around Margaret Anne, had a gleam in his eye.

"I have some good news for you also, Mags," he said.

"Let's have it," she mouthed, the words coming a little better now.

"I heard from the lawyer. The store has made an offer of twenty thousand dollars compensation for your injuries. But he says you shouldn't accept that. He figures it's worth an awful lot more. That's something to look forward to, huh?"

Margaret Anne tried not to grin because of the pain in her jaw. But she just couldn't help herself.

Some minutes later a pretty, black-haired nurse arrived with lunch and a course of pills for Margaret Anne.

"Mmm, that smells good. We'll leave you for a while to rest and get something to eat ourselves. Sound good, Gordon?"

"Sounds good. We won't be gone long, Mags."

They got their trays of food and found a quiet table for two in a corner of the cafeteria. As they sat down facing each other, Neil's face assumed a rather serious expression. Gordon was quick to notice it.

"Something's up," he said anxiously. "Is Mags okay?"

Neil put down his knife and fork and, looking directly at Gordon, replied, "Margaret Anne, or Mags, as you call her, is fine. But her father is terminally ill and has, at best, a year to live. He has cancer of the liver."

Gordon was shocked.

"I can't believe it," he said. "He looks so strong and healthy. What a shame, such a nice man."

"Now," Neil continued, "he's going to break the news to Margaret Anne today. And he's asked me to be there when he does. The thing is that Gráinne is not aware of his condition."

"I see."

"So I want you to come up with some kind of excuse to get her out of the room for a few minutes. I'll give you the nod."

"God, Neil, this is going to be a bad shock for poor Mags. I hope she's up to it."

"She'll have to know sooner or later. And Eoin and myself have decided that now is the best time. If she gets unduly upset we can always give her some medication."

"I suppose. But still ..."

"You see, Gordon, the thing is, her father is depending on her to take care of her mother. We hope that when the time comes Margaret Anne will be braced for it, and will be strong for Gráinne."

"I wish there was more I could do."

"You'll have a big part to play in helping Margaret Anne. I know that you'll be there for her."

"Of course I will," Gordon replied adamantly."And of course I'll think of something to get her mother out of the room. I do hope everything works out without too much grief."

"Dr Neil O'Grady to Reception," the announcement intoned loudly through the intercom.

"That will be Eoin and Gráinne now," Neil said, rising.

Gráinne was thrilled to see Neil and Gordon, and she embraced them both warmly.

"You look great," Neil remarked, admiring her fashionable, floral dress.

"Would you believe she's still trying to convince me she's not Mags's sister?" Gordon asked with a wink.

"Come on now, you two. Flattery will get you nowhere. Let's go and see the patient."

Margaret Anne was delighted to see her parents, and, although she found it difficult to converse in comfort, she did well, improving every time she spoke. Gordon thought she looked radiantly happy and his heart broke for her, knowing the news she was about to receive.

Neil thought that Eoin looked dreadful. His skin tone appeared more yellowish than it had before, his eyes were deeply sunken, and he kept biting his lower lip. Was he in pain or was it the strain of the ordeal that lay ahead of him? Neil decided that it should be got over with as quickly as possible. He caught Gordon's eye and nodded briefly.

Gordon took the cue at once. At the first lull in conversation he asked, "Would you mind coming for a little stroll around the grounds with me, Mrs O'Dowd? There's something I'd like to discuss with you."

Surprised, Gráinne looked to her daughter for some clue. Margaret Anne smiled knowingly. She knew exactly what Gordon had to say. They had discussed it before the accident. He sure doesn't waste much time, she thought, as Gordon ushered her mother through the door.

A moment of tense silence followed, with Eoin looking from Neil to Margaret Anne, then shifting nervously in his chair. He suddenly wished he had not decided to do this at all. It was one of the hardest things he'd ever had to do in his life. Neil, noticing how taut he was, decided to take the initiative. He pulled his chair a little closer to the bed and spoke.

"Your father has something to say to you, Margaret Anne. It's a hard thing to say and I know he's finding it difficult. You will help him won't you?"

She looked at her father and suddenly knew that something was radically wrong. He did look so drawn, so tired. It was more than just being tired after the trip. Instinctively, she took his hand.

"Of course, Dad. God knows you've helped me enough. Now it's my turn."

Her voice came out strained but distinct. Eoin was encouraged, and he shifted one last time and searched for the best words.

"I'm not quite sure of the best way to put this," he began. "But I guess there's only one way, and that's to give you the facts as they are."

Margaret Anne was apprehensive now, and Neil held her hand tightly.

"I'm very ill, Margaret Anne," her father went on.

"In fact, to be honest and truthful with you, I'm dying."

The words hit her like a bludgeon and her face went white as she stared at him for a moment in horror and disbelief. She hadn't expected to hear anything as bad as this. Then suddenly a huge flood of emotion welled up inside her. She burst into tears, leaned forward, and fell into his outstretched arms. She thought her heart would collapse, so great was the sadness and grief she felt.

Deeply moved, Neil watched Eoin hold his grief-stricken daughter as the tears streamed down his own face. Neil decided to leave them alone for a while and he slipped quietly out of the room.

After what seemed like ages, Margaret Anne dried her eyes and, making an effort to take control of herself, asked the inevitable question.

"Is it cancer?"

"Yes, of the liver. I've got maybe twelve months."

"Oh Dad," she cried bursting into tears again, "I can't take it, it's not fair. Oh Dad, I do love you, you know I can't bear the thought of losing you."

"Try and be brave now, darling, for me. Will you please? You know I'm depending on you to take care of Mum. She doesn't know yet and I don't know when and how I'm going to tell her, if ever."

Margaret Anne suddenly understood his great concern for her mother, that same concern which had always annoyed and irritated her. He must have known for quite some time.

"I'll try my best, Dad," she uttered faintly, crying all the while. "But what will we do without you?"

"Don't think of that for the moment. Now, we'll just take every day as it comes and be grateful to have it."

Eoin paused and looked thoughtful.

"I'll have to go back to Ireland as soon as possible. Your mother, of course, will be glad to go. But I was hoping that you might come too. Would you?"

Before she had an opportunity to answer, Neil returned.

"Gráinne and Gordon are on their way back," he said. "We have to be cheerful now whether we like it or not."

Gráinne came through the door first, her face flushed with excitement. She went straight to Margaret Anne, and throwing her arms around her, exclaimed, "Congratulations darling, I'm so happy for you. It's the most wonderful news I've heard for a long time. And I know Gordon will be an excellent husband, just like your father."

Eoin looked in amazement from mother to daughter and then to Gordon, who stood at the end of the bed, his eyes fixed on Margaret Anne.

"I haven't been asked for my daughter's hand yet," Eoin remarked jovially.

"May I please, Mr O'Dowd," Gordon asked.

"Certainly, son, with my blessing," he said, moving to the foot of the bed and embracing Gordon.

Neil was extremely happy for all of them, and kissing Margaret Anne affectionately, he said, "I never thought I would see this day, Margaret Anne O'Dowd. But I must compliment you on your choice. He's a great guy."

"I know. And you'll never guess where we're going to spend our honeymoon," she announced to everyone. Gordon hadn't a clue. He gave Margaret Anne an odd look. This had never been discussed.

"We're going to Ireland," she continued, taking her father by the hand and looking lovingly at him.

"And we may even decide to stay there."

"Sounds great. I'll second that," Gordon replied, realising immediately what had prompted her decision.

Seizing on the opportunity of the moment, Eoin took Gráinne in his arms and twirled her to him.

"And how would you like to go to Ireland for a long holiday, Mrs O'Dowd?" he asked.

Gráinne's eyes lit up and her face became transfigured. "Oh Eoin, you know I would love it. You're so wonderful to think of it. Thank you so much."

Neil beamed, amazed everything had worked out so well.

"I'm proud of you kid," he whispered to his cousin. "You've made your father a very happy man."

Margaret Anne looked up at Neil and smiled, blinking happily through her tear-filled eyes.

PART 2 IRELAND

CHAPTER 13

There it is -- the dawn on the hills of Ireland, Eoin said to himself, peering through the window of the jet as it descended towards Shannon Airport. Six weeks had passed since the dramatic day at the hospital. In spite of everything, Eoin felt strangely happy and at peace. The fear and anxiety ebbed away and in their place came this lovely feeling of security, even exhilaration. He'd come to terms with the inevitable. It was great to be home. For how long, he didn't know, but he did know that everything would be easier now. Gráinne was so happy that she looked ten years younger. And Margaret Anne and Gordon were like love's young dream, even if the duty-free Irish whiskey contributed something to this mood. Neil's surgery had been masterful; Margaret Anne looked just as beautiful as she did before the accident. Imagine, just three days married, and about to embark on a new life in Ireland. It was great to have his family all around him. He felt so happy that he could hardly hold back the tears. He had made his will and tidied up all the loose odds and ends. Neil was selling the house and furniture as arranged. He had nothing more to do now but to live every day to the full, in the knowledge that when his time came, his wife and daughter would at least be well taken care of and, above all, that they would be at home among their own. How and when to tell Gráinne was the only dark spot. But that would work itself out too, and he put it out of his mind for the moment anyway.

Alana and Fergal were at the airport to meet them. Alana was Margaret Anne's godmother and Gráinne's older sister. She had once been with the nuns and she still bore a very pious demeanour. Her hair was now silver, but she was still attractive. She was a woman who had soldiered through a great many problems, all the while willing to give of herself completely to anyone in need. With her was her son, Fergal. Eoin could hardly believe how time had flown, for Fergal had grown up into a fine young man.

As soon as the welcomes and greetings were said, Fergal whisked them all away in his powerful, black Mercedes. Gordon sat in the passenger's seat, excitedly taking in his first glimpses of this land about which he had heard such wonderful stories.

"Hey, the grass really is fresh and green," he remarked.

"We pay dearly for it," Fergal replied. "It rains here quite a lot, you know."

"No shortage of water then, I guess."

"Lord no. Sure, we could supply the world with water. As a matter of fact, there are a few very profitable companies at the moment exporting mineral water."

"It seems a pretty good idea," Gordon said.

Then, turning back to Margaret Anne, he continued, "We might even get into that ourselves, what do you say, Mags?"

"I can't say a thing right now. I'm too scared."

"Scared? What are you scared of?"

"Well, I don't think these little roads are meant for this kind of speed."

Fergal turned back briefly with a tight smile on his face.

"You think I'm driving too fast, do you?"

"I sure do, you're spooking me."

"It's a fast-moving little country, you know," Fergal remarked suavely.

"The days of the horse and cart are gone."

"And the pigs in the parlour," Margaret Anne quipped.

These yanks think they're the only people who drive fast cars, Fergal thought. In fact, they think they're the only ones who are civilised at all. Well, I've shown them, he thought, pleased.

Alana knew exactly what was in her son's mind. This was typical of him. She had noticed herself that his driving was particularly speedy, and she had seen Gráinne squeeze Eoin's hand nervously.

"Take it a little easier, Fergal," she said.

"It's not very comfortable for any of us."

Men are such babies, she thought. Do they ever stop to think that there is only one difference between driving and speeding, and that's putting your foot down on the accelerator? She was tired of telling him that.

Fergal reluctantly complied, but he then turned on the stereo full blast, putting an end to all conversation.

"Is this it?" Gordon asked as Fergal stopped the car outside the pub at Clover Road. It had been freshly painted in bright yellow, and a large Guinness sign stuck out very prominently.

"Yes, this is Gran's birthplace," Margaret Anne replied.

"It's from one of these windows she escaped to marry Grandad. She'll tell you all about it as only she can."

Gordon had already heard a lot about the family's past. How Margaret Anne's grandmother, Peggy O'Flaherty, had defied her father's wishes and married Hugh O'Grady, the local school teacher. He'd heard about their children, Alana who left the nuns to help her sister Deirdre, who'd been abandoned by her husband. And then their was Mags's mother, Gráinne, who had married Eoin O'Dowd, the son of the Garda sergeant. Eoin 's work had taken them to California when Margaret Anne was just a little girl.

Peggy hadn't been so excited for a long time. She had never in her wildest dreams expected to have her favourite daughter back with her to care for her in her old age. Bríd was very good to her undoubtedly, but strangers are never the same as your own. And anyway, Bríd had her hands full with her daughter, Jennifer, who was absolutely spoilt. But what a godsend that child had been. Gavin had been in the depths of depression after Margaret Anne took Georgie away from him. And then miraculously, in the face of the doctor's pronouncements, he and

Bríd had conceived a baby. Peggy reckoned that that baby had saved Gavin from a life of deep depression, though God knew he could still be moody at times. Gráinne's Eoin, on the other hand, had always been a lovely fellow. And he would be very useful in the bar. Wasn't the Lord very good to her?

Gavin, however, wasn't at all keen on meeting Margaret Anne. He could never forget the cruel, heartless way she'd taken Georgie away from him. Nor could he forget the insulting remarks she'd made to Bríd and himself. Bríd had told him that she had changed a lot since then, but he doubted that somehow. Her type never change. He pitied the poor chap that had married her. He must be a fool, or else a very brave man. He was glad she was only staying the one night.

And when Gavin saw her walk in the door less than half an hour later, greet everyone, and then ask about the baby, he thought she had the same sickly smile she'd worn those long months before. She was admiring Jennifer now, cooing at her. Anyone would think she liked babies. Where was her own baby?

"And how are you, Gavin?" she asked him casually.

He had to steel himself even to answer her.

"I'm fine, and how's little Georgie?"

"Georgie? Oh, little Bikram, you mean. We had his name changed and I forgot for a second," she said, giving a little laugh.

"Very funny," Gavin said bitterly.

Margaret Anne's eyes flashed.

"That's certainly more than I can say for you," she shot back.

"Well, I'm not funny anymore, that's life. I'm twenty-seven years old and I'm a cripple in a wheelchair. And you almost crippled my heart when you snatched Georgie from me. That's not funny, nor amusing, nor cute."

"No, but then again it's not as pitiful as you would like us to think it is. Stop feeling sorry for yourself. Haven't you an adorable little daughter?"

"I thank God for her every day of my life, but I'll never forget Georgie."

Gordon was worried and uncomfortable now.

"That's enough, Mags," he said, putting his arm around her tenderly, stopping her from letting loose another retort.

"Let's not spoil this joyful occasion by bickering."

Some moments later, Alana met Eoin's eyes. They were lifeless and sunken in his head. He looked dreadful. Meeting Alana's concerned gaze, Eoin knew instinctively that she knew. In a way he was relieved. He could count on Alana to keep Gráinne sane.

"You must all be tired," Alana said brightly, addressing the four travellers.

"As soon as lunch is over, you all ought to go upstairs and have a nap."

They retired to the spacious, pine kitchen and Bríd served up a delicious lunch of wholesome Irish stew as only she could cook it.

"This sure is good," Gordon said.

"Compliments to the chef. And a very pretty one if I may say so."

"Thank you." Bríd replied, blushing profusely.

"I'm glad you enjoyed it."

"You ought to teach Margaret Anne how to make it," Peggy added.

"No need Gran, I will never be your typical Irish housewife. As long as I have a tin and a tin-opener, I'll be okay."

Peggy was shocked to the core and she blessed herself.

"In the name of all that's good and holy," she exclaimed, "what kind of a wife are you going to be?" Then turning to Gordon she added, "I pity you, young man. You'll surely die of malnutrition."

"No need to worry about me. I'm well able to take care of myself."

"As indeed all men should be," Margaret Anne remarked adamantly.

Gavin was sure she'd darted a look at him when she said this. He could feel another strong wave of temper mounting inside him. On the verge of exploding, he turned his wheelchair and left the table.

Fergal, sensing another uncomfortable scene, caught Margaret Anne's attention.

"What are your plans?" he asked his cousin.

Reluctantly she turned her attention to him.

"Oh, we leave first thing tomorrow morning on our delayed honeymoon. Gordon's hired a car and we will travel all around the country."

"That's lovely. But I was referring to your long-term plans. I mean what do you both intend to do for a living?"

"We're not quite sure yet. I have a substantial sum that I was awarded as compensation for an accident I was in, and Gordon has about twenty thousand to invest. We'll probably start up some business."

Fergal was all ears now; he loved business discussions.

"As it happens," he said eagerly, "I know of a small hotel in a little town on the west coast of Cork. The bank is selling it. You should get it quite reasonably for cash. And I can tell you that it would be an excellent venture. I've looked into it myself."

"That sounds great," Gordon said, excited now.

"How do we get to it?"

Fergal got pen and paper and drew a little map explaining the route to them in detail.

"If you need any more help give me a ring. Meantime I'll contact the auctioneer handling the sale and arrange an appointment for you. Here's my telephone number, give me a ring sometime tomorrow."

When lunch was over, Fergal excused himself to go to a business meeting.Bríd tidied up, Peggy and Gráinne remained deep in conversation at the table, and Margaret Anne and Gordon went upstairs for a nap.

Though Eoin looked more tired than any of the others he did not join his daughter and son-in-law. Instead he walked to the front door with Alana, and, as they stood facing each other, there was a moment of tense silence.

"How are you feeling, Eoin?" she asked.

Eoin hesitated. He wanted to be quite sure she meant what he thought she meant.

"I know all about it," she said, her eyes dark with sudden pain.

"Neil told me, I hope you don't mind. I'm so stunned by the absolute finality of it. I don't know what Gráinne will do without you."

Crestfallen, Eoin spoke softly to his wife's sister.

"She is my biggest worry right now. But I know you'll help her and try to give her the strength and courage you've always had. I always think of the way you soldiered on against all the odds. Then of course she'll have her mother. And look at them," Eoin said smiling.

"They're as thick as thieves. She hasn't left her side since she arrived."

"You know I'll do everything I can to help," Alana said.

Eoin nodded and sighed deeply.

"I hope Margaret Anne is all right now that she's married to Gordon. But I do worry about her. She can change so quickly, and she's so unpredictable. You will keep an eye on her, won't you?"

His voice held a slight tremor. He looked away for a second as if to hide his face.

"You know I will, Eoin," Alana replied.

"They'll be all right. You're tired now and things appear worse than they are. Have a rest and we'll talk later."

As he lay in bed that night, his eyes closed, relaxing, he realised Alana was right. Taking in the cool, Irish air, he could feel the tensions easing away. He felt as though he were regaining his strength after five agonising months of stress. Not to mention the trouble and agony before that with Margaret Anne. If the truth were known, life hadn't been normal for years and years. But now he was able to relax and feel nothing. He looked at Gráinne, sleeping peacefully beside him. He held her hand and smiled. He was safe at last.

CHAPTER 14

The little hotel was just as Margaret Anne and Gordon dreamt it would be. It stood aloft in an acre of verdant gardens overlooking the harbour in the peaceful picturesque fishing village of Kilbawn. Its architecture was clearly Victorian, with light, sand-coloured stone work which seemed to have been recently restored. The rooms at the front had their own private balconies with panoramic views of the sea and surrounding countryside. It had thirty bedrooms in all and it appeared to be in an excellent state of repair and decor.

After first viewing the place, they had decided to spend the night in one of the rooms. Sunlight peeping in through the heavy, gold curtains woke them up in each other's arms. Gordon looked down on his new bride with great happiness, watching her face to see the same sentiment mirrored there. He admired the long, graceful lines of her lovely face, the big, blue eyes, the tousled, blonde hair.

"I really meant what I said to you last night. I love you, Mags."

"And I love you too."

She believed she really meant the words and that she had no regrets for having married him. He was part of her troubled, turbulent past, but it was he who had lifted her out of the mire.

"What do you think of our hotel?" he asked her.

"It's so cosy and welcoming. I love it, really I do. I think it was meant for us."

"We'll go for it then. What do you say?"

"Yes, all the way. The minute I walked inside the door here I could feel a warmth, a soothing atmosphere. It's delightful."

The dining room, with its pale, pink-and-white decor, was heavenly. Fresh air drifting through the open window brought with it the salty smell of the sea mingled with the sweet scent of the flowers that grew in riotous colour in the garden outside.

"I can't wait to have this place for our very own," Margaret Anne said with an eagerness and excitement that Gordon hadn't seen for a long time.

"Let's ring Fergal right away and get the wheels in motion."

They left the table, walked hand in hand through the lobby, past the reception desk, and into the phone booth on the left.

Fergal wasted no time and early in the afternoon the proprietress received a telephone call from the auctioneer asking her to give them the grand tour of the place.

Rose Broderick was clearly a lady, with a most warm, friendly manner and an attractive, soft brogue. In her early forties, she had the most magnificent head of dark, auburn hair, and large, hazel eyes that shone in her face, even if there was a certain tinge of sadness about them.

The more they saw of the hotel, the more they liked it, and the more anxious they were to purchase it. The rooms were furnished with a simple, yet distinctive elegance. The accent definitely was on warmth and comfort, with an easy grace that lent itself to a relaxing holiday hotel.

Gordon loved the traditional, Irish paintings that hung on the walls and the large vases of colourful flowers and foliage from the garden, which were almost always the focal points in the lovely, sun-drenched rooms.

The pièce de resistance, they thought, was their own cosy, self-contained flat in the basement. It had everything in one small area. Gordon was lost in amazement at the manner in which every inch of space was used to maximum advantage. It had one fully-fitted bedroom, and a long, narrow sitting room, with a most attractive dinette in the corner beside the window. In the other corner of this room, there was what looked like a large press from ceiling to floor with cream-coloured louvre doors which, when opened, displayed a mini-kitchen with all mod cons. They were both enthralled with the whole set-up.

Later, in the oak-panelled bar with the soft, mellow light emanating from its large yellow lamps, they sat with Rose to discuss the financial details.

"I may as well be honest and candid with you," she began.

"It's breaking my heart to have to part with this place, it has been in my family for generations and I love every inch of it. It's part and parcel of my entire life."

She paused for a moment as if overcome, and they were reluctant to ask the question that was foremost in their minds.

"You see," she continued, "my husband died a year ago, leaving very substantial debts. And the bank is selling. I have no other choice. He was an alcoholic, you see, and a pathological gambler. And you know what a disastrous combination that is."

They both knew only too well.

"I'm so sorry," Margaret Anne said.

"What will you do now?" Gordon enquired with great sympathy.

"I'm not quite sure yet," she replied. "I have a nineteen-year-old son, Kieran, who has just finished training as a hotel manager, and, well, I was hoping that whoever bought the place, might give him the job. He knows the business like the back of his hand."

Gordon and Margaret Anne conferred with their eyes for a second and then in one voice they agreed. They could see the relief in Rose's face.

"I could help out myself at busy periods or whenever the two of you wanted time off. I'm going to live with my sister who is only about five minutes walk away."

"We will probably take you up on that offer quite often," Gordon replied.

"Would you like to meet Kieran then?" she asked, with pride in her eyes.

"Let's buy the place first and then we can arrange to do that," Gordon answered.

"Have you any idea what the asking price is?" Margaret Anne enquired.

"Between ourselves now," she whispered, "they are looking for a quarter of a million. But I know they'll sell for two hundred and twenty thousand. Take my word for it, you're getting the bargain of a century at that."

Later that night they spoke to Fergal on the telephone.

"You couldn't go wrong at the price," he said.

"It's a very attractive investment. I'd nearly be interested myself if you weren't in before me."

"What do we do next?" Gordon asked eagerly.

"I'll arrange for you to see a solicitor and you can pay the deposit. Then we'll have the contract drawn up and fix a closing date for the sale."

"But what about the balance of the money?" Margaret Anne whispered to Gordon.

"I heard that," Fergal said impishly. "There will be absolutely no problem, leave that to me, I'll arrange a loan."

Gordon smiled as he hung up and conveyed the message to her.

"Are you happy now?"

"You bet. Let's ring Mum and Dad. A bit of good, exciting news is what he needs right now to lift his spirits."

They got through to Eoin, and he was truly overjoyed at the news.

"Mum and myself will come down for a week or two when you've settled it. We want to be the first names in your visitors' book," Eoin said.

"I'd really like that, Dad," Margaret Anne said wistfully. "And believe me, this place is a haven of peace and tranquillity. You're going to adore it."

"What's the name of the hotel?" her father asked.

"The Kilbawn Inn", but that doesn't do it justice at all. So Gordon and I have decided to rename it 'The Harbour Star'. We think that would sell it better."

"Yes, I think so. It sounds a lot nicer anyway. The other is too mundane and commonplace."

"That's exactly it, Dad. By the way is Mum there with you?"

"No, she's hardly left Gran's side since she came home. They're inseparable, the two of them. I don't know what they find to talk about."

"That might be a good thing considering --" Margaret Anne abruptly stopped herself. What a terrible thing to say. She could have eaten her words. How insensitive of her.

But Eoin knew exactly what she meant.

"You're perfectly right, Margaret Anne. I was thinking the very same thing myself. Believe me, their closeness gives me great peace and consolation."

"You're so brave, Dad. I really love you."

Eoin sensed she was in tears.

"Hurry up with that hotel of yours. I want to be there before this fine spell ends. You have no idea how much I'm looking forward to it."

After long negotiations, the sale was finally closed and they proudly took possession of The Harbour Star. On that particular day they were booked out, but fortunately the Queen Maeve suite had been vacated unexpectedly the previous morning. They'd kept it free to entertain and accommodate the family, who were coming that evening for the celebration dinner and house warming party. Eoin, Gráinne, and Peggy would remain on for a week or two with the suite all to themselves.

"That's the least I could do for them," Margaret Anne had said to Gordon.

"It will probably be their last holiday together, poor Mum and Dad."

Kieran Broderick had been at his post since early morning and he went about the work with an air of confidence and poise, getting things in perfect order. Gordon worked with him, and Margaret Anne could see that he was eager to learn the business. By evening Rose and Kieran between them had everything under control with absolutely no hassle or disruption.

Kieran was the image of his mother -- tall, very handsome, and with the same thick, wavy, auburn hair. He looked a great deal more mature than his nineteen years. He was immaculately groomed, and Margaret Anne thought he had a definite aura of class and distinction about him. This made him admirably suited for the job.

It had been a glorious day with temperature in the twenties, and even now several of the guests were seated on the round, metal tables scattered on the white terrace which stretched along the side of the hotel facing the sea. Gordon and Margaret Anne mingled among the guests, making their acquaintance and wishing them a happy holiday. They didn't realise it was so late until they heard the Angelus ring from the little church in the village.

"God, is it that time already?" Gordon exclaimed with surprise. "Time flies when you're busy."

"It sure does," Margaret Anne replied, looking up at the sky which looked as red as fire.

"A red sky at night is a shepherd's delight," she recited. "It looks as though the heat wave is set to continue. Dad will be thrilled."

"What time are the folks arriving?" Gordon asked her.

She came down to earth then as she replied with a touch of panic, "Oh no, they'll be here in a little less than an hour. We had better go and get dressed for dinner."

She decided to wear the red, silk cocktail dress that Monique had selected for her on that eventful day in San Diego.

"You look absolutely delectable, sweetheart," Gordon remarked, sweeping her into his arms and kissing her.

"Thanks a lot, love. But look at you -- the hotel tycoon. You look great."

She smiled in open admiration as he strutted around the room, modelling his steel-grey suit, sparkling, white shirt, dark, wine dicky bow, and highly-polished, black shoes.

"We've got to look the part," he said with a broad smile as they made their way to the lobby for a quick drink before the arrival of their guests.

"It's so exciting," Margaret Anne said, her eyes sparkling. "I can't believe we've done it."

Gordon raised his glass to hers.

"Here's a toast to The Harbour Star, and to my very special star, Mags O'Dowd-Edwards."

CHAPTER 15

From the moment they were all seated around the large, rectangular oak table in the dining room with its bright colour scheme of primrose and beige, Margaret Anne knew the evening was going to be a great success. There was an air of cheer and gaiety. Everybody looked well and appeared to be in top form. This was a very special party, and glancing around her at her family, Margaret Anne could not help thinking how elegantly dressed the women in particular were.

Blue had always been her mother's colour, and tonight's blue, linen dress gave her an almost youthful appearance. Peggy looked aristocratic in the dark, mauve, silk suit which sharply contrasted with her silver hair.

"You look stunning, Gran," Margaret Anne exclaimed in genuine admiration.

"That's more than I can say for you," came the unexpected reply. "You ought to go to your room and dress yourself properly."

Only Gran could get away with this, Margaret Anne thought, taking a deep drink before replying.

"Why? What's wrong with this dress? It cost a fortune."

"It's immodest and indecent and certainly not befitting a hotel proprietress."

Margaret Anne would have lashed out at anyone else. But not at her Gran. She refilled her glass and drank deeply. The alcohol was going to her head. She had been drinking so little lately, she was unaccustomed to it.

Alana was embarrassed by her mother's sharp comment, especially when she saw the puzzled, hurt look on Gordon's face.

"Don't take any notice of Mum," she said. "She has a strange sense of humour."

Margaret Anne was grateful for Alana's diplomacy. And how well she looked. Margaret Anne had never seen her look so glamorous. She wore a cream, silk suit with soft, peach dots. She'd been accompanied by her sons Fergal and young Eoin. Bobby, her youngest, had stayed behind with her husband, Ian, who hadn't been too well of late.

The party had already finished four bottles of champagne when the tall, burly chef, dressed in full regalia, wheeled in the bain-marie. It was laden with delicious food which was served very efficiently by one of the younger waitresses.

Everything was superb. Garlic mushrooms served as the starter, followed by thick, creamy, mushroom soup. Roast leg of lamb with mint sauce followed, along with a multitude of fresh, green vegetables and floury potatoes in their jackets. Desserts were selected from a trolley full of everything imaginable, after which the diners retired to the lounge for coffee and drinks.

Gordon who had been deeply engrossed in conversation with Fergal and young Eoin, suddenly noticed that his wife was in a pensive mood. It wasn't like her to resist dancing to the music that streamed forth from the stereo in the corner of the room, especially when it was playing a collection of dance music from James Last. He excused himself and went to her.

"A penny for your thoughts."

She looked up glumly and, he thought, somewhat drunkenly, at him. He took her by the hand and leaned closer to her.

"The party is a great success and everyone is having a wonderful time. There's no need to worry, darling."

She smiled at him.

"I know. But I'm just thinking of Dad and feeling a bit sad," she said, her voice slightly slurred. "There's always something, isn't there?"

"Put that thought out of your little head. Look at him enjoying himself. I've never seen him in better form. I think he's even tipsy. He was hitting the champagne pretty hard, just like his daughter."

Before she could respond or object Gordon steered her out to the dancefloor. She smiled and they danced in silence for a few minutes.

"Those two certainly are in love," Alana whispered to Bríd.

Gráinne overheard her and smiled.

"He really is the best thing that ever happened to Margaret Anne, and I have the greatest respect for him," she said.

Eoin, sitting beside her with another glass of champagne, agreed wholeheartedly.

"Only for him, God alone knows what would have become of her."

Peggy noticed Eoin's loud, slurred speech.

"I've never seen you drunk before," she said. "Don't tell me you're starting now."

"Let him alone, Gran," Fergal interjected. "A few drinks won't do him any harm. And anyway, it's a very special night."

"You should have a few yourself, Peggy," Eoin teased her.

Peggy primly tapped the Pioneer pin on her dress, saying, "I'm not likely to break the pledge now, at this hour of my life."

But, over the next several minutes, as Eoin continued his prodigious consumption, Fergal became concerned. He took his mother and twirled her around in the centre of the floor. After a few seconds he whispered down to her.

"You ought to do something about Uncle Eoin. I don't think he should be drinking so much, especially when he's not accustomed to it. And in his condition."

"I think you're right," Alana whispered back.

"It's almost time for us to be going home anyway. It's late enough and we have a fairly long drive. He'll settle down to bed as soon as we go."

After the dance Fergal broke the news to Margaret Anne.

"Don't be such a spoilsport," she sulked as Fergal buttoned his coat. She felt as if the alcohol was just beginning to kick in, and here was Fergal trying to opt out.

"It's after midnight and we have quite a drive home and a very early start in the morning," he explained.

Margaret Anne was about to answer, but he intercepted her reply with an affectionate kiss.

"It's been a wonderful evening, and thanks a lot."

Everyone gathered around and conveyed their thanks and best wishes for the future success of the hotel.

"You should be in your bed long ago, Mum," Alana said to Peggy as she left.

"Gráinne will settle you down now, and herself and Eoin should do likewise."

Margaret Anne continued to drink long after her parents and grandmother had gone to bed.

"I think you've had enough now," Gordon said at last.

He almost had to lift her down to their apartment in the basement. She was sound asleep in a matter of minutes while he lay there awake, staring at her, feeling disappointed and frustrated. This wasn't how he had expected the night to end. It was definitely an anti-climax. Gordon couldn't sleep. His feelings ranged from excitement to apprehension about the day ahead. He hadn't realised there was so much to be learned about running a hotel.

Margaret Anne slowly awoke to the eerie sound of an ambulance siren in the still of the night. Still half asleep, she stretched her hand over to rouse Gordon, but all she could feel was an empty space.

"Damn it," she said to herself.

"I must have crashed out and he's still up there having a ball."

She hadn't the faintest idea how she got to bed or how long she'd been there. But she could hear quite a lot of activity upstairs. Why not get up and rejoin the party? She badly needed another drink anyway. She switched on the bedside lamp on the locker beside her and the little digital clock on the radio flashed five-thirty. Maybe she didn't need that other drink. She turned over again and closed her eyes. Better sleep this hangover off, she thought. Tomorrow would be a busy day and she'd need to have her wits about her.

Some time later the telephone rang and she leapt up with a start. She was about to replace the receiver on the cradle and then take it off the hook, but her curiosity got the better of her.

"Who is it?"

"It's me, Gordon."

"Where the hell are you? And what do you want at this unearthly hour?"

"I'm at St Joseph's Hospital here in Cork. Your father took a very bad turn. He's in critical condition. You'd better get up here at once."

"Why don't you come and get me?" she said, feeling too sick to care, not to mention to drive a car.

His message had not really registered.

"There isn't time, Mags. For God's sake, gather yourself together and get here as quickly as possible."

It was all beginning to sink into her numbed brain now. The ambulance, the activity upstairs, the urgency in Gordon's voice.

"My God!" she exclaimed. "You mean he's dying?"

"Yes, Mags, I'm so sorry. Get Rose or Kieran to drive you, but don't delay," he said and the phone clicked off.

Her mind was in a state of turmoil and confusion, bordering on absolute disorientation, as she sat at the side of the bed staring into space like someone paralysed. She didn't hear Kieran knock several times on the door, nor did she hear him opening it and walking in.

"Mrs Edwards?" she heard his voice and she looked up at him standing there puzzled and embarrassed.

"Get ready quickly, I have the car running outside the door."

"Oh God, yes" she replied, coming to herself, springing into action. Kieran looked away as she leapt into a pair of slacks and a t-shirt, before running madly up the stairs.

The scene at her father's bedside was calm and peaceful. One of the nursing sisters stood on his left, reciting the Rosary, and Gordon stood beside her. Gráinne sat at the other side with her hands clasped in one of Eoin's. To Margaret Anne's surprise, she seemed unexpectedly composed.

Margaret Anne replaced Gordon and the sister at her father's bedside and took hold of his free hand. Bending forward, trembling, she kissed him. He opened his eyes momentarily, smiled, and then he was gone. It was just as if had hung on until she came.

The sister waited for a few minutes, then, having made absolutely certain that he was dead, she looked to Gráinne and Margaret Anne.

"I'm so very sorry," she said softly and with great sympathy in her voice. "Mr O'Dowd has gone to heaven. I will leave you alone for a while to grieve in private."

Margaret Anne went to her mother and the two women fell into each other's arms, sobbing bitterly and uncontrollably. After some time they felt Gordon's arms encircling them and Margaret Anne looked up, the big tears still flowing down her cheeks.

"It was better this way," Gordon remarked.

"He didn't suffer and he had a beautiful death."

"In God's name why didn't you call me?" Margaret Anne hissed up at him, angry now."I should have been here with him."

"I tried, but you were out for the count, and there wasn't time."

"He had only just begun his holiday," Gráinne cried. "And he was looking forward to it so much."

She broke again into sobs that racked her body.

"I don't know what I'll do without him," she cried, looking down on him. "Oh Eoin, why did you have to go? Why did God take you away from me?"

"Hush now," Gordon said kindly, holding her shoulder."You have Mags and I, and we'll take care of you."

Gráinne barely heard his word. She was reeling from the shock. She could not believe this horrendous thing had happened. He had been so well yesterday and so happy last night. She felt as if she was living some horrifying nightmare to which there was no end. She wept and wept for the husband who had been her life, who had taken care of everything, and whose only concern had always been her happiness. She wept for herself also. What was to become of her now? How was she going to cope with life without him?

Margaret Anne put her head in her hands and countless memories took her back in time for a few minutes. She hadn't exactly been a model daughter, and she had caused her father a lot of worry and trouble. She was just about to make it up to him, but she didn't get the chance. He'd wanted so much to live. He'd fought so hard to keep going. Every minute was precious to him, he had told her that so many times lately.

"Come on now," Gordon entreated, "you both need a rest." He led them reluctantly, one on each arm, out through the door.

Neil flew home for the funeral, and as he stood by the graveside his mind swung back to the day Eoin had signed the will in his presence. How neat and orderly he had left all his affairs. He was glad he had completed the sale of the house and furniture, and he considered one hundred and fifty thousand dollars a handsome price. Gráinne would have a nice little nest egg. And that was exactly what Eoin had wanted. Even in death he had her interest at heart. Neil had the bank draft in his breast pocket, together with a copy of the will.

He'd discussed it only with Alana and they both had decided to allow a few days to elapse before broaching the subject. Poor Gráinne was out of her mind with grief at the moment.

CHAPTER 16

Bad times followed for Gordon and Margaret Anne. Margaret Anne resented the fact that Gordon did not wake her that night and inwardly she felt guilty because she knew he was right, she'd been in no condition to get up. Her father's death deeply unsettled her. Though she thought she'd be braced for it, she wasn't. She thought of all the hurt she'd caused that good man and grew depressed and bitter with herself. She began to drink very heavily and avoided Gordon. His concern repulsed her. What good had all her father's concern for her done him? Couldn't he see she wasn't what he'd built her up to be? She was just a terrible, selfish, miserable person.

Seeing that his concern only drove her further away, Gordon threw himself into work at the hotel. He was determined to become absolutely familiar with every aspect of the business. As the days and months passed by his hours grew longer and longer and it was rarely that he returned downstairs to the apartment before ten o'clock at night. He resumed duty at six every morning and there was no deviation from this relentless schedule. Work was his salvation now, the only therapy for his troubled mind. But despite his hard work, the world-wide recession was having a big effect on the tourist trade. The hotel was struggling along.

He seldom saw Margaret Anne these days except for fleeting interludes, and at those times she was usually too drunk to communicate. Her grief for her father had erupted into a terrible anger that seemed to be eating her up inside. This reaction was in marked contrast to her mother's. Gráinne, in fact, was making an excellent recovery, taking great solace from her religion. Margaret Anne had shut him out completely and Gordon daren't make any gesture, not even one of consolation towards her. Her only comfort now came from a bottle and he had no option but to stand idly by and watch her yet again go down the wrong road. Rose Broderick was a tower of strength to Gordon. Not only did she and Kieran keep the hotel running like clockwork, but she seemed concerned for him as a person. She had that serene, calm maturity that made him wish far too often that he had married somebody like her.

It was in desperation that he asked her to fill the vacant space at his table tonight. He urgently needed to talk to someone and somehow he felt that she would listen sympathetically and understand. Sitting with her face to face, Gordon realised that she was truly beautiful. In the candlelight her face had become mellow, erotic, and intriguing. Her sensuality was tantalisingly visible through the shimmering, shell-pink dress she wore. He was, without warning, overwhelmed by an insatiable desire to seduce her. And yet he was also aware that she was totally oblivious to his feelings. Clenching his jaw tightly, he determinedly switched his mind to business.

"We don't seem to be getting that great a response to my little marketing campaign in the United States," he said, shifting uneasily in his chair.

Rose patted him on the hand.

"It was a bad season for everyone. Things will pick up next year."

"I'm sure they will," Gordon said flatly, failing to muster the enthusiasm he didn't feel.

Rose was quick to notice.

"You're worried. I know you are," she said with a tenderness that almost brought tears to his eyes.

"It's your wife, isn't it?"

"I guess you've noticed," he replied, and then took a long drink from his glass of wine.

Rose was so sorry for him. He was such a thorough gentleman, and so sincere and genuine. She knew he adored his wife, and she was well aware of the heartache and frustration he now suffered. Nevertheless it was kinder to him to be frank and honest, rather than to console him with false platitudes.

"Yes," she answered softly.

"And what is more, Kieran has had quite a few complaints from staff and visitors about her bizarre behaviour."

Gordon dropped his fork. This was something he hadn't expected to hear.

"What do you mean? I know she's drinking like a fish, but what else is she up to?"

"Well," Rose continued, "for one thing she is making a nuisance of herself in the lounge, invading the privacy of couples who are trying to have a quiet, relaxing drink. That would be bad enough if she were sober, but you know what it's like listening to silly gibberish from a drunken person. Then, if she doesn't get an enthusiastic hearing, she becomes aggressive. She publicly denounced Ireland and the Irish race the night before last and then she began to sing "The Star Spangled Banner". Lots of people walked out and they haven't returned."

"My God," Gordon exclaimed.

"This is dreadful. She'll ruin us. Something must be done at once."

"If it's any consolation at all to you," Rose continued, "I have been through it all with my husband. It was a living nightmare, and believe me, I know what you're going through. You can count on my help if you need it. But the sooner the problem is tackled the better, because if it isn't Kieran won't stay."

"What? Why?"

Rose hesitated a moment. She truly detested the thought of upsetting him any further, but a stitch in time saves nine, she reasoned.

"Well Gordon, when Kieran came to his room last Saturday night, he was horrified to find her in his bed. And I can assure you he had a terrible problem trying to ward off her advances."

"Did he?" Gordon cried, alarmed now.

"I know he did because he came to my room in a very distressed state. He actually slept on the floor there."

"Here he is now," Gordon said as the young man approached the table.

"May I have a word with you outside, Mr Edwards?" he whispered discreetly.

"Certainly, Kieran," Gordon said, slightly embarrassed to see the young man. He then excused himself and left the table. He knew there was something amiss.

"What's wrong, Kieran?" he asked as they headed to his office.

"It's Mrs Edwards," Kieran mumbled, looking upset and embarrassed. "She's just telephoned from the Garda station in the village."

"The Garda station! Was there an accident? She's not hurt is she?" Gordon asked, terrified.

"No, no. It's nothing like that. I didn't quite understand a lot of what she was saying. She wasn't really making much sense."

"In other words, she was drunk."

Kieran blushed and nodded.

"That's right, Mr Edwards. It seems that there was a foreign ship in the harbour, and it was raided by the Guards. They found drugs and everyone aboard was arrested ... including Mrs Edwards."

"Oh my God, that's all I need now," he said, rushing through the door like a demented man. Please God, don't let Mags be back into the drugs.

More than an hour later he returned with Margaret Anne, now relatively sober. Her face was pale and her hair dishevelled. She was dressed in black, skin-tight pants and a long, white, sloppy blouse.

Gordon dragged her by the hand past the reception desk, where Rose and a few guests stood talking, and downstairs to the apartment with a sense of urgency. He locked the door behind them and she threw herself down with a thump onto the bed.

Gordon picked up the telephone and she lolled her head towards him. Her eyes held a questioning look but they were soon to flash with anger.

"Rose, I won't be available for the remainder of the evening. I've got more urgent business taking care of my junkie wife," he said, throwing Margaret Anne a look.

"Ask Kieran to take care of the cash for me, and he might drop down the cash book later. Thank you, Rose."

Gordon's disgust made his voice dry and expressionless. He turned to face her, but before he had an opportunity to utter a syllable she sat up erect on the bed with a ferocious look on her face.

"Why the hell should you be so angry? And what authority do you have to demand the cash book?"

She was shouting and crying at the same time.

"You're getting too big for your boots. Remember this, Gordon Edwards: I am my own woman and always will be. And don't forget that it's my money that got us this hotel. I own sixty-three percent of this place."

Taken aback by this last statement, Gordon walked across the room and stood for a moment with his back to her. She was still yelling.

"I want you to know once and for all that I'm in charge around here and I'll give the orders from now on. Is that clear?"

He turned towards her again and in a quiet, calm, self-controlled voice replied, "Perfectly clear, and you know something, sister? You have just made me feel as small as two cents. I take your point. You're the boss and I'm the boy."

By the time he'd finished he sounded crestfallen and exhausted.

"Oh, so you're feeling sorry for yourself now? You can't take it, can you? But you didn't consider how I felt when you dragged me across the lobby and then phoned your precious Rose in a deliberate effort to belittle me."

She tried to sound sarcastic again, but tears stung in her eyes.

Gordon thought he could detect a slight softening in her face.

"It's not fair Mags," he said, "not at all. You refuse to treat me like a real person, never mind your husband. Did it ever occur to you that I am a man and that I like to feel like one, and that I have some needs here? You refuse to believe that I love you and that I can't continue to live like this."

"And you refuse to believe that I no longer dabble in drugs. I promised you that a long time ago and I haven't broken my promise."

"Then what were you doing aboard that ship?"

"Having fun, having a few drinks, nothing else apart from doing some business."

He was startled now. She wasn't dealing was she?

"What kind of business?"

"Hotel business," she quipped. "I've got a booking for a party of thirty French fishermen for the month of September," she said, a note of triumph in her voice.

She has us booked out for September? That would be perfect. It would settle most of the financial problems. He couldn't help smiling, looking at her there. She wasn't doing drugs at all. She was drumming up business for what would have been a slow, costly month. Look at her sitting on that bed, her blazing beauty, her boundless energy. What was she doing with a man like him? Despite it all, he still realized he was lucky to have her.

"You're a star, Mags. You always were a star."

"Well, what happened to my manager?"

"That's all I ever wanted to be. I should have trusted you. I'm sorry, so very sorry, darling about what I did up there."

He took her in his arms and kissed her.

"I love you Mags O'Dowd-Edwards. My God, I really do, and I always will."

"And I love you, too," she whispered, pulling him close to her.

She was in his arms clinging to him, saying his name over and over again, and he held her close to his body. He kissed her again and again as he had wanted to do for the longest time, fiercely and passionately. She returned his kisses with an ardour that made him realise that she wanted him too. He looked into her eyes and they were full of the same yearning and desire that he felt. There was no going back now, they must make love at once. He turned off the lamp, undressed quickly, and, in a blaze of passion, slid into bed beside her. They gave themselves to each other in a way that they had never done before and their bodies became united as one.

As they lay there entirely contented and locked in each others arms, they heard the gentle tap on the door.

"Who is it?" Gordon asked.

"It's me, Kieran. I have the cash book."

They looked at each other and smiled. Gordon thought her face was radiant.

"Take them away, Kieran. They are not important now, tomorrow will do."

Gordon continued to hold her close to him, and she felt as though she were enveloped in a cloud of peace and happiness. The tension that had been building up in her since her father's death had at last disappeared.

"I feel so happy tonight," she said. "I think I've finally accepted Dad's death."

"I'm so glad, darling. And this is only the beginning of our life together. I want you with me all the way, Mags. Together we will greet the guests, plan all sorts of wonderful functions, and we will sit together at our own little table at dinner each night."

"And all I'll have to do is look beautiful and exotic?" she asked teasingly.

"No, but you sure won't have any trouble with that part of it."

CHAPTER 17

Weeks drifted by and Gordon and Margaret Anne grew in love for each other, living and working together in perfect peace and harmony. Their zeal and enthusiasm in the management of the affairs of The Harbour Star were a powerful force in transforming the little hotel from a small Irish holiday inn into a haven for visitors from all over the globe.

Rose was most agreeably surprised at the great change for the better in Margaret Anne. She had become the perfect hostess, thoughtful, polite and courteous, and she was loved and admired by all, staff and visitors alike. Gordon was truly proud of her, and Rose saw that the tense, strained look had disappeared completely from his face.

"I can't believe she's the same person. My God, she's just as adorable as she was horrible," Rose remarked to Gordon as they drank their morning coffee in his office.

"How on earth did you manage it? I wish I had known your secret years ago. There's no doubt about it but you are some operator."

"I had absolutely nothing at all to do with it," Gordon replied emphatically. "It was her very own decision and will power. I know Mags, and I can tell you she's a woman of fierce determination. When she does something she does it all the way. Unfortunately that can work two ways. However, so far so good, and believe me, I am grateful and very relieved."

Rose had a wistful, faraway look in her eyes.

"You're lucky, and you deserve it," she remarked.

Suddenly Gordon felt his heart go out to her.

"Cheer up, Rose," he said, putting his arm gently around her. "One never knows what could happen next. Lives can change in the flicker of an eyelash."

A week later, on September 1st, Margaret Anne's contingent of thirty French anglers took up residence, causing quite a stir in the hotel, and indeed in the village at large. Every fisherman for miles around was employed to take groups of them out in their boats. Anything at all that could float was in use. There was an air of affluence and prosperity in Kilbawn never before known.

Everyone returned in the evening to the hotel bar where the events of the day were thrashed out in detail in French and English, with a word of Irish thrown in here and there for spice. The merriment and carousing went on into the early hours of the morning.

Mick the Mouth, as he was known, was the Harbour Master. As such, he got a percentage of the takings from every boat that went out. He scrupulously collected his money each night. Before the fishermen had the opportunity to put a pint to their lips, he was there with his little red notebook, where all their dues were carefully calculated. Mick was small, with a head of black, curly hair and a small beard, along with a very rotund belly. Mick the Mouth was known for his endless repertoire of unlikely stories and anecdotes, all of which he swore to be true.

Although the Frenchmen didn't understand half of what he said his antics alone amused and entertained them. Pierre de Lancel was sitting beside Mick one night, watching him. Like most of his compatriots, Pierre was slim and fit. He looked at Mick in disgust.

"Mon dieu," he exclaimed, "you have large abdomen. You look just like someone ten months pregnant."

Mick stood up and stuck his belly out proudly.

"That cost me a fortune of money I'll have you know, sir. And there's plenty of room in there for more porter, so open your little black purse there now, froggie lad, and call for a drink."

Pierre quickly changed the subject but Mick the Mouth soon interrupted: "I will sing for you, froggie lad, a song about the bridges of Paris."

Mick then gathered himself, making sure he had everyone's attention, and launched into song:

> There's nothing under the bridges only water
> And that's too weak for me.
> I want a good, strong Guinness.

Peals of laughter followed and when they'd subsided, Dinny Mulcahy stood up.

"Let's drink a toast to Bobby Twomey," he said, lifting his pint glass. "His missus had her tenth son today."

"Dix enfants?" Pierre exclaimed in horror. "Poor woman."

"What's the matter, boy?" Mick asked. "Sure, isn't that what he got her for?"

Pierre was totally nonplussed.

"You have very funny way of seeing things," he replied.

Johnny Moore came through the door at that moment, still dressed in his navy wedding suit, the red carnation still fresh in the lapel.

"Any more boats wanted?" he asked Mick.

"'Tisn't boats you should have on your mind tonight, man. Shouldn't you be on your honeymoon?"

"That can wait. I need the money."

"You need your head tested," Mick said with a wink of his eye to the others.

"Why so?" asked Johnny.

"Well, we all know your new bride is no oil painting, and that's putting it mildly."

"It doesn't matter a damn," Johnny announced.

"Hasn't she eighty acres of land? And anyway, sure, she won't be going out much."

The Frenchmen looked in amazement from one to another and they didn't know whether to laugh or cry. Just then Rose appeared on the scene.

"Come on now, gentlemen, please. I think it's time to call it a day."

Pierre rose and kissed her hand.

"Anything for you, dear lady."

Jean Duvalle, however, sat gazing at Rose like someone hypnotised. Jean was a tall, handsome, slender man in his late forties. He'd been smoking his pipe quietly all night, not saying much, but taking everything in. He was absolutely and totally smitten by Rose.

Most of the men in the party had fallen for her, but none among them was as hard hit as Jean. He sat gazing out of his bedroom window into the moonlit night long after he had closed the door behind him. He was so unhinged by love that he eventually found himself lying in the bed with his clothes still on. Never had he seen such a woman. Never could there be another. He would die if he couldn't spend the rest of his life with her. He got up and paced around the room, ending up, after several circles, back at the window trying to plan his strategy. He must propose to this woman before he went back to France because there must be many others trying to get her to marry them. In order to win her he had to get her to himself without wasting any time. For he knew, with the instinct of a man in love, that the six others who shared his table at dinner had fallen under her spell as well. And wasn't Pierre kissing her hand just a few hours ago? Panic suddenly gripped him. What if she were married already? He would kill himself. He hadn't see any man with her. And what man would have left her side? But he didn't even know her name. All he knew was that he wanted her and that he must have her.

Early the next morning, Jean knocked on the door of Gordon's office.

"Come in," Gordon answered, and Jean entered, looking fresh and fit, pipe in mouth. "What can I do for you Monsieur Duvalle?"

"Oh, it is nothing really," he said casually. "But that lady, the tall lady, the one with the big, beautiful eyes, what name has she?"

"That must be Rose, our manageress," Gordon said, curious now.

"Has she, how you say ... "

"A husband?" Gordon smiled.

"Oui."

"No, Monsieur Duvalle. Her husband died a few years ago. She's a widow."

"Merci, mon dieu," he sighed, relief written all over his face. Gordon was simultaneously horrified and amused by this sentiment.

"Pardonnez," Jean said. "What a terrible thing to say. I mean I am glad for me. You see, Mr Edwards, I love her."

"I can't say I blame you for that. She's an extremely attractive woman. But what do you want me to do for you?"

Jean hesitated a moment, puffing his pipe frantically.

"I was wondering if maybe you could set up appointment for me with her."

"Ah now, Monsieur Duvalle, I think you would be far better off if you did that yourself. I've always heard that you French are a romantic breed. But I'll tell you this -- I have the strangest feeling that Rose will be delighted."

"Really?"

"Really. Oh by the way, just on the chance you're interested ..."

"Oui, oui?"

"She has the whole day off tomorrow," Gordon said, winking.

"Merci, then tomorrow I must ask her to be my wife," the Frenchman said, rushing out.

Before Gordon could fully absorb what he'd said, the telephone on his desk rang. It was Ron Harte from Gold FM in San Diego.

"Hi, Ron," Gordon said, "what a pleasant surprise. How did you know where to find me?"

"It's a small world and I have my sources."

"It has to be our mutual friend Charlie. He's the only one in California who knows my whereabouts."

"Right first time."

"Anyway, what can I do for you?"

"Nothing really, but I think I may be able to do something for you that might be of mutual benefit to both of us."

Gordon was interested now.

"Okay," he said. "let's hear it."

"A few friends of mine are involved in a new film company, they call themselves Phoenix Film Incorporated. One of them is good friends with Charlie. Anyway, they had this Irish project they were considering, and they were looking for sights, and Charlie mentioned where you were. Anyway, they sent a scout out there a few months back, you probably never even noticed him."

"We did have a lot of people pass through. Oh wait, it must have been that weird guy, Rob Pekkanen, I think his name was. Kept walking around and peering at everything real funny."

"That'd be him. And he was so impressed that they want to bring a film crew over and do some preliminary shooting."

"You're kidding."

"Nope. And I was hoping that you might be able to accommodate them. Money is no object."

"How many are there?"

"Twenty-five all together. And they need to come in three weeks time."

Gordon was elated.

"That would be just perfect. And believe me, there is some beautiful scenery here."

"So Pekkanen's been telling everyone."

"Hey thanks, Ron. I owe you one."

"Before you get too grateful now, don't forget that I'll be looking for a commission."

"You're a tough cookie, Ronaldo. What sort of deal are you looking for?"

"Let's say five percent."

Gordon puckered his eyebrows.

"That's a bit much, Ron. Our margins are tight enough."

"Pile it onto the bill, man, there'll be no problem there. Have we a deal?"

There was a moment of silence before Gordon said, "It's a deal."

He couldn't wait to tell Margaret Anne. This was some scoop, and perfect timing as well. She was in the kitchen discussing the dinner menu with the head chef. Gordon popped his head in the door.

"Mags, can I have a quick word with you?"

"I'm almost finished now," she replied. "Anything wrong?"

"No, no. I'll be downstairs in the apartment when you're ready."

The coffee was just bubbling in the percolator when she came rushing into the kitchen.

"Well, what's up?" she asked with an air of anticipation.

"I have two very exciting items of news," he said and handed her a mug of coffee. "The first concerns Rose, and the second ourselves. Which do you want to hear first?"

"About us," she replied without hesitation.

"I had a phone call just now from Ron Harte," he continued and her eyes opened widely in amazement. "He is sending us the cast and crew of a film which is being shot here in Kilbawn. There are twenty-five in all and they will be arriving in three weeks time for at least two months."

She literally jumped for joy.

"Oh my God, that's fantastic!" she shrieked. "This is our big breakthrough. We've got it made. Oh Gordon, I love you," she cried, throwing her arms around his neck.

"Don't thank me, thank Ron. I did nothing but accept."

"Good old Ron," she said. "I'll forgive him for firing me. It's really wonderful."

"Before you go off into an ecstasy, let me tell you about Rose."

"Oh yes, Rose," she answered, but he could see that her mind was spinning at the speed of light, and she was planning ahead already.

"Monsieur Duvalle has fallen madly in love with her. He's going to propose to her tomorrow."

"You can't be serious?" she remarked, highly amused.

"I'm deadly serious, and so is Monsieur Duvalle I can tell you."

"Do you think she'll accept?"

"I have the strangest feeling that she just may."

A small silence then fell between them, and as Gordon looked at her he was struck by the note of mystery in her expression.

Then arching her brows, she cleared her throat and said softly, "Do you want to hear a third item of news?"

He was slightly puzzled now. He didn't quite know what to expect.

"Of course I do."

"I have a strange feeling ..." She stopped, took a sip out of her coffee and, after a slight hesitation, finished quietly. "I think I'm pregnant."

Gordon looked dazed for a moment, and then a broad smile broke through and his blue eyes were alight with joy. His excited voice echoed the expression on his face when he exclaimed, "Mags, my darling Mags, this is the most wonderful news of all. In fact the best I've ever had in my life."

Reaching out for her, he brought her into his arms, kissed her tenderly and then held her face gently between his hands. After a moment he murmured, "You said you think. Aren't you sure, baby?"

She looked up into his eyes and nodded.

"All the signs are there. When I see the doctor I know the answer will be positive."

"Let's go right away," he said.

"Take it easy, there's plenty of time. But I promise I'll go before the week is out."

"Oh Mags, isn't it just marvellous?"

"I'm glad you're so happy about it," she said, her voice gentle and tender.

"Of course I am. Why wouldn't I be?" Then he became serious. "Aren't you?"

"I'm thrilled. But I was just a little worried about the running of the hotel."

"That takes second place to our son," he said, truly exhilarated.

"Our daughter, you mean."

CHAPTER 18

At exactly seven-thirty that evening, showered, shaved, and smelling of expensive aftershave, Jean Duvalle sat in the foyer of the hotel, looking around him anxiously, hoping to come across Rose. He was immaculately groomed, wearing well-tailored, grey pants, dazzling white shirt, with navy dickey bow, and a navy blazer. He had finished his drink and he was toying nervously with his glass, looking at his watch at very regular intervals. Suddenly he saw her, and his heart missed a beat. She came through a door behind the reception desk and she looked lovelier than ever in a pale, green silk dress. With it she wore two strands of exquisite pearls and large pearl earrings. Jean got up and walked quickly towards her like a man besotted with love.

"Oh, here you are, Rose," he said, giving her a warm, loving smile and almost bowing before her. "I was waiting for you. I need to talk to you in private."

Rose wondered what on earth could be wrong, but in a professional manner she kept her poise and smiled politely back.

"Of course, Monsieur Duvalle. Why don't we go to the Residents' Lounge. No one's there at the moment and it's nice and comfortable."

They sat on a small, floral couch in the alcove of the large bay window.

"Well now," Rose smiled, "what can I do for you?"

He looked at her for a second, thinking how beautiful she was. Her smooth, velvety cheeks were slightly flushed and there was a radiance about her which he found absolutely breathtaking.

"I find it très difficile to say this," he began slowly, "but I think you are a most charming lady. And, dare I say it, a very loveable one. I would like it very much if you could come to dinner with me. I understand you have a day off tomorrow."

Rose was smiling outwardly, but within she was in turmoil. She really didn't know what to do or say, and she began to feel shy and awkward. She had to admit she was flattered. He was, after all, a very handsome man, distinguished and noble-looking. And he smoked a pipe. She had always admired men who smoked pipes. It couldn't do any harm to go out with him. She decided to take a chance.

"I see you have been doing your homework," she replied.

"Yes, I spoke to Monsieur Gordon and he told me. Be my guest, please do."

"All right then," she agreed. "I'll meet you at the end of the drive beside the hotel gate at seven-thirty tomorrow evening."

"Oh thank you, thank you," he exclaimed, taking her hand and kissing it

The next evening they drove out of the village in Rose's silver Renault Five.

"I see you drive French automobile. That is good omen I think," he grinned.

"That may be so," she replied, slightly embarrassed. "But it's a grand little car."

"Where are we going?" he asked.

"There is a small, very select restaurant a few miles down this road. It's famous for its cordon bleu cuisine. I'm sure you'll like it."

"C'est magnifique," he exclaimed as the waiter led them to a table for two in the cosy, plush restaurant, with its soft, rose-coloured lights and lilac decor. Jean seated Rose in a comfortable chair and ordered a bottle of the very best champagne. He plucked a white flower from the little vase in the centre of the table and pressed it into her auburn hair, fussing over her like a man in the throes of love, which indeed he was.

She accepted his attentions in her characteristically warm, dignified fashion. She noticed several people in the restaurant glancing surreptitiously in their direction but she wasn't in the least bit perturbed. She felt they made a very striking couple with an air of great glamour about them. He poured her a glass of cool champagne and another, and by the time the starter was set before them they were both relaxed and talkative.

"You must tell me all about yourself," Rose said.

He wiped his mouth with the pink linen serviette and, resting his elbows on the table, began.

"Mon dieu, but it is a long story. Where do I begin?" he asked, his voice simmering with emotion.

"Just try the beginning," Rose replied, smiling.

"Yes," he continued. "I was born in the most beautiful corner of this world in Provence, where my father owned a large vineyard. He was French and my mother was Spanish, such a beautiful woman with always a smile on her face. She could cook the most delicious meals that I have ever tasted."

"Are they still alive?" Rose interrupted.

"No, no, regrettement. It was very sad. My father was killed when he fell from his horse and my mother, who adored him, died within a year. She was, of course, heart-broken."

Rose was deeply touched, especially as she could see the tears well up in his brown eyes.

"I am so sorry," she remarked.

"Ah well, c'est la vie. Anyway," he continued, "I am only child and I inherited the vineyards, hundreds of hectares of glorious vines. I have continued to work them and I do very nicely."

"Did you marry?" she asked, her heart pounding for some strange reason.

"Yes. I married Jenette when I was twenty-two. But just two years ago she was killed in an airplane crash with my sweet eighteen-year-old Claudine."

"Oh, you poor man," Rose exclaimed, "that's such a very sad story. What a tragic life you've had."

"I am lonely now, my Rose, so very lonely and all alone in my very big house. Maybe I am too old, but I am asking you to be my wife. I would give you a beautiful life and I believe we could be very happy. I have been looking for someone like you. Je t'aime, I love you, Rose."

She was totally overcome.

"This is too sudden, far too quick. I only met you properly last night and I couldn't possibly say that I love you. I think you're a very kind, loving man, but that's not enough."

"That is enough for now," he assured her. "I know I can make you love me. Please say yes, and come home with me to Provence."

"Well, for starters," she continued, "I cannot go anywhere or do anything for at least two or three months until the film crew have gone. I couldn't walk out on Gordon at such a very busy time."

His face fell and she detected a note of agitation in his voice.

"But why, you are free my dear. You have no ties. Three months is such a long, long time."

"You must be patient for a little while," she told him tenderly. "Let me give all this some thought. Meanwhile we can get to know each other."

"But I go back to France in two weeks. You could be snapped up when my back is turned."

"There is no fear of that," Rose laughed.

"We'll keep in touch. And sure, we still have two weeks to go."

"You will give me some kind of promise before I return," he begged.

"Yes, I think that might be possible all right" she said, smiling lovingly at him. He lifted his two hands in a gesture of extreme delight.

"Quelle nuit!" he exclaimed aloud. "L'amour c'est belle."

CHAPTER 19

Two weeks later, on September 30th, Jean Duvalle and the rest of his party left the Harbour Star. As the private coach moved slowly away from the front door he waved through the window at Rose, blowing kisses frantically until the coach had gone through the gate and out of sight. There were tears in her eyes as she waved back, but the large cluster of diamonds on her left finger didn't go unnoticed as it sparkled in the brilliant, Autumn sunlight.

"Oh Rose, it's so beautiful," Margaret Anne exclaimed in wild admiration. "It must have cost a fortune."

She threw her arms around her.

"Congratulations. I'm so happy for you."

"Me too," Gordon added as he embraced her affectionately. "You sure deserve it. Let's hope you find happiness second time round."

"Thank you. I feel sure I will," she replied. "You have no idea what a wonderful person Jean really is."

"What does Kieran think of your whirlwind romance?" Margaret Anne asked.

Rose smiled ruefully.

"Well, to be honest with you, he was none too happy at first. He told me I was acting like a teenager. But it's my life, and I don't intend to throw away the chance of happiness with somebody else."

"You're perfectly right. Never mind him, he'll come round when the initial shock wears off. And anyway, from what I've seen, he won't be long after you himself."

Rose smiled. She knew Kieran was in love with Eithne Whelan, the young girl recently hired to assist him.

"I hate to interrupt this conversation," Gordon remarked, "but there is quite a lot of planning and organisation to be done before our film crew arrives. The director is due here the day after tomorrow to survey the place, and as we all know, yanks are pretty demanding people."

The director, Nick Benson, was six feet tall, fifty years of age or more, and extremely handsome in a rugged sort of way. He had a commanding, though calm air about him. It was obvious that he was a man accustomed to power who could use it with very little fuss or effort. His assistant director, Guy Petrassi, was a sturdy man in his early thirties. He was olive-skinned with jet-black hair and the typically warm-blooded look of an Italian. He had a distinct aura of vigour and authority, with his prominent, hawk nose and ferocious eyes.

"It's nice to be in this beautiful, peaceful corner of the world," Nick Benson smiled at Rose, as she handed him the visitors' book to sign.

"You're very welcome. I hope you find everything to your satisfaction," she replied giving him two room keys. "These are rooms one and two, the very best in the house. You'll have a panoramic view of the sea and surrounding countryside. If there's anything else you require, please let us know."

"We won't have much time for gazing through the window," Guy Petrassi interjected as he motioned impatiently to the porter to bring up the luggage.

Nick Benson turned to his colleague, "You go on ahead, Guy, and let me sort out a few details with, I didn't get your name?"

Rose blushed a little.

"Rose Broderick, but just call me Rose."

"Okay, Rose. Here are a few things I need right away," he said, glancing at the large, gold watch on his wrist.

"It's three o'clock. I would like everything to be in order before the day is over. I expect to begin work at six tomorrow morning."

"Would you care to step in my office?" Rose replied and she led him through Reception and into her small office at the back.

"Let's see now," he said as he sat outside her desk on the black, leather chair. He pulled a little, red notebook from the inside pocket of his wine-coloured blazer. Rose walked around her desk and sat down, her face now assuming a serious expression. This man meant business.

"In order of importance," Nick continued, "here is what I require. Firstly, a large private room within the hotel which we'll use as a meeting place for executives and the more important actors and actresses."

Rose could see no problem with that. The Queen Maeve Suite was the perfect answer.

"Next, a fairly large jeep, capable of carrying up to six passengers. Then a spacious hall, if possible close to the hotel, which we'll need as a studio, and the rest I think I will be able to take care of myself."

"I'll get working on these items straight away" Rose replied. "And I should have some definite information for you at dinner tonight. I have a few ideas already. I can't see any problem with them."

He thanked her and rose to leave.

"By the way, Mr Benson," she asked, "when do the remainder of the crew arrive?"

"Oh yes," he answered. "I'm glad you asked, because they'll be here Thursday, that's three days from now, and I'll require twenty five extra rooms. The equipment should be here before then, all going well."

As dawn was breaking the following morning, Guy and Nick could be seen, binoculars thrown casually over their shoulders, getting into the large jeep to suss out the area. Gordon travelled with them to point them in the right direction.

"What sort of film is it going to be?" Gordon asked just for the sake of conversation.

Nick began to explain.

"It tells the story of the ups and downs of a typical Irish family before they decide to emigrate to America."

"I see," Gordon replied. Was it his imagination or was Nick Benson looking at him strangely?

"So only part of the shoot is to be done here?" Gordon asked, trying to deflect the director's penetrating stare.

"A little less than half and half," Nick answered, dropping his gaze at last. "There will be a further six months or so of work to be done at our own studios in Hollywood."

"Stop here," Guy interrupted excitedly, pointing to six small cottages which nestled at the foot of the hill overlooking the harbour.

"I like this, I like it. I think it might be just the perfect spot."

They got out of the jeep and scrutinised the area, Guy referring every now and then to the notes the earlier scout had drawn up.

"We have a choice of four pubs, my God you Irish, and there is the church and two shops all in close proximity. We've hit the jackpot first time."

Nick took a quick look at the script and then had a long, searching look through his binoculars.

"There isn't a hospital," he remarked, and then he turned to Gordon and gave him that same piercing look.

"Is there one in the village?"

Gordon's face fell. He thought they would have to go elsewhere.

"No, I'm afraid not and the nearest one is thirty miles away."

"No problem," Guy replied. "We can construct that scene in a studio. There's not much to it anyway."

Gordon had succeeded in getting the community hall for that purpose at a very handsome rent. It suited admirably and the committee were more than pleased with the deal.

Within two weeks everything was in full swing and the little village of Kilbawn was yet again a hive of activity, with plenty of money floating around. Decorators and tradesmen of every kind had been employed to give the cottages, pubs and shops a face-lift, inside and out, and the locals were in high spirits. Margaret Anne was aglow with excitement from the moment the cast and crew arrived.

"What do you think I should wear for dinner tonight?" she asked Gordon as she emerged from the bathroom, wrapped in a soft, pink bath towel.

Relaxing on the sofa, sipping a glass of ginger ale, Gordon turned to her with a vibrant smile and a toss of his blonde hair.

"Whatever you wear you will look adorable, Mags, my love."

"But I want to look my very best tonight to impress these movie stars."

"I bet there isn't one of them could hold a candle to you," he said, getting off the sofa and hugging her tightly.

In the end she wore her cream, silk tunic with the plain, rounded neck and a straight, black, silk shirt. She looked and felt elegant as Gordon led her to their own table in the dining room, careful to put her in the best seat with the best view of the room.

"First a glass of champagne," he proposed and ordered from the waiter.

"Tell me who everybody is," Margaret Anne implored him. "You met them all today."

Gordon looked about him discreetly and pointed out the actors and actresses, as well as to the camera men, make-up people and, of course, Guy and Nick. Margaret Anne cast a quick glance at each one as he did so.

"I've never heard of any of these people," she whispered. "None of them are famous."

Disappointed, she sipped her wine and gazed around the room, her huge eyes wistful, yet alert.

Nick, Guy, and Tony -- the camera man -- were seated together at a table not far from them.

"Take a look at that girl," Guy directed his dinner companions. "The one up there with Edwards."

The three men turned their heads slightly and examined Margaret Anne from head to foot.

"She's incredible, " Guy continued.

"She must be his wife," Nick said, an edge in his voice.

"He sure is a lucky man," Tony exclaimed, studying her features with the eye of a professional camera man, contemplating how it would fare under the lights.

He had seen too many extraordinary eyes lose their lustre when the camera was focused on them. He was thinking hard now, however, and Nick could read his thoughts.

"You want to test her, don't you, Tony?"

Tony's eyes lit up.

"You bet I do. I have the strangest feeling she'd be perfect."

"Have you got a part in mind for her?" Guy asked Nick.

"Well there's the part of Amanda."

"What about Shirley Cooper?"

"I talked to her agent again today. They're still holding out for more money. I did have her earmarked for Amanda, but then again it won't hurt to test Mrs Edwards there. One never knows and there is nothing signed yet."

"It's settled, then?" Tony asked with enthusiasm.

Nick looked at Guy and a nod of agreement passed between them.

"I'll go and introduce myself," Tony said. "I'll try and arrange it for tomorrow afternoon. Okay with you, Nick?"

"Fine, Tony, just perfect."

Greeting Margaret Anne, the first thing that struck Tony was that her accent was as distinctly American as his own. Gordon was slightly resentful of the invasion of their privacy, but courtesy and the age old adage that the customer is always right forbade him from displaying any outward sign of annoyance as Tony stayed on talking.

"Your hotel is very pretty, and the food is delicious," Tony went on. "My compliments to you both."

"We're glad everything is to your satisfaction," Gordon said somewhat icily, hoping he would leave them alone to get on with their meal. Gordon also had the strange feeling that Nick Benson was giving him that strange stare again, but he dared not turn around to see.

Abruptly Tony pulled out a chair.

"Do you mind if I join you for a while?"

We don't have much choice, Gordon said to himself, as he replied in a slightly peevish tone of voice, "Feel free."

From then on Tony addressed Margaret Anne exclusively.

"Why'd you come to this country?" he asked.

"I was born in Ireland," she answered. "My parents are Irish, and well, I guess the savage loves his native shore."

"I guess so," Tony chortled.

He then grew quiet, but stared intensely at her until she felt quite uncomfortable. "I have another question to ask you, Mrs Edwards," he said at last.

"Fire away."

"Well," he continued, "my boss, Nick Benson, was wondering if you would do a little screen test for us tomorrow afternoon. That's if you have a few minutes to spare. It would be an experience if nothing else."

"A screen test?" she exclaimed in delight. "I'd love it, it would be so exciting."

She turned to Gordon, her eyes glowing like stars. But she saw immediately that he was none too pleased, and her face fell.

"Don't you think that that would be very tiring for you in your condition? And anyway what would be the point?"

He looked directly at Tony now.

"Is this test with a view to casting my wife in some role?"

"Could be," Tony replied, "could very well be."

"Do you mind if we discuss this privately for a while?" Gordon asked. "We'll give you an answer before you finish dinner."

"No problem," Tony replied as he got up and left the table.

Margaret Anne was furious. Her blue eyes blazed with anger.

"How many times have I told you that I do my own thinking? I can answer for myself. I'm not a child, and I'm nobody's property. How dare you humiliate me like that?"

Gordon threw his hands up in the air in despair.

"Cool it, Mags. I'm sorry, really I am. I just thought it might not be wise."

"I'll decide that for myself, thank you. And I can't for the life of me see what harm it could possibly do. Are you afraid I might get a part and become famous, could that be it?"

"No, that's definitely not it, Mags. But have you forgotten you're pregnant? And that you may not be able to take the part even if you do get it?"

"I'll worry about that if the occasion arises. Meantime I'm going to do that screen test whether you like it or not."

Gordon knew that it was useless to argue the point any further.

"Okay, Mags, now simmer down and let's forget this unpleasant interlude. I guess I was wrong. You go and do your own thing, love, and have fun."

She left the table at that juncture and notified Tony of her decision. When she returned to Gordon she was smiling again.

"He's picking me up at two tomorrow," she announced.

Gordon felt the resentment building up inside himself again. Just because some jerk saw her, and she appealed to him, he waltzes over and asks her to do a screen test. And now she's over the moon. Women, how vain and easily flattered they are.

"You do realise that it will take all the afternoon and well into the evening," he ventured to comment.

"It's my time, not yours," she replied curtly and defiantly.

CHAPTER 20

When Tony led Margaret Anne into the hall the following afternoon she was flabbergasted at the total transformation that had been wrought within. A huge stage had been erected at the very top and there were props, cameras, lights and yards and yards of cable everywhere. Nick, Guy, and some other executives sat on red plush chairs close to the stage and the strong aroma of their cigars pervaded the atmosphere. The little annexe formerly used as a kitchen had been magnificently converted into a make-up room, the floor and walls covered in brilliant, white tiles.

Large mirrors were everywhere and underneath each one was a shelf laden with boxes of cosmetics, combs and brushes. Rita Hughes, the make-up woman, was tall and willowy, her blonde hair swept up in a large bun. She was charming and friendly, putting Margaret Anne immediately at ease.

"There isn't much work to be done with you," she smiled, taking Margaret Anne's jacket and seating her on the white, leather armchair in front of the mirror.

Standing behind her, running her fingers through her hair, examining her closely all the while, Rita was very impressed.

"You definitely have the most perfect features I ever did see. Look at those eyes, and that beautiful, curving mouth. Nature has been very kind to you, my love."

Margaret Anne was elated.

"Oh thank you, Rita. That's nice to hear from a professional like yourself."

"We will, however, have to perform certain tricks, just so that the camera will be kind to you," Rita said, patting dark shades of base in the sockets of her eyes, with little dashes of mascara, rouge, and lipstick here and there.

Outside the door Tony was waiting for her.

"Exquisite, magnificent," he exclaimed, leading her to where Nick and Guy were sitting.

"We're so happy that you accepted our invitation," Guy spoke for both of them.

"I hope I'll be okay," she replied nervously.

"You'll be just fine," Nick assured her. "There's no need to be apprehensive. Just be your own beautiful self and you should be perfect."

Guy produced a page of script.

"Sit here beside me," he said "and I'll show you what you will read. Right here where it's marked 'Amanda.' I'll read the others. Let's just have a nice, natural, little chat, you and I, that's all."

As soon as she was familiar with the reading, he led her onto the stage, and seated her on a high stool.

"Now as soon as I give the signal, you will begin, understood?"

"Yes," she replied, trying to keep as calm and composed as she possibly could.

Guy gave the order, counting down to zero. Then a bank of powerful lights smashed on and she could hardly focus on the lines before her. Taking a deep breath and a firm grip on herself, she began to read, totally oblivious to the cameras and spectators until Guy finally barked, "Cut!"

The lights were turned off and it was all over.

"You were fabulous," Nick said, coming towards her with a beaming face.

"I've never seen anyone so natural. And not a single break. It was perfect. You're a born actress."

Margaret Anne literally shook with excitement. Never before had she felt so alive, so totally exhilarated.

"How would you like to play the part of Amanda? It's yours for the taking," Nick announced.

"You mean it, you're actually offering me a role in this film?"

"That's right -- and a very important one at that."

She suddenly remembered something and the thought cast a very serious cloud over her face.

Nick observed the change instantly.

"What's the matter?" he asked. "Is there a problem?"

She was reluctant to answer for a moment but then she realised there was no point in hiding it.

"I'm pregnant," she said in a low voice.

Both men eyed her curiously. It was Guy who spoke first. "When is your baby due?"

"The beginning of next May."

"What a shame," Guy said, "that's just about the time we are due to shoot in Hollywood."

"Ah well," she replied, "that's the way it goes. Thanks for the offer all the same."

It was obvious, however, that she was bitterly disappointed, as indeed were they. Nick thought hard. There had to be some way around this. She was so sensational that she was bound to be a hit.

"Wait a minute," he said finally.

"Are you thinking what I'm thinking?" Guy interrupted excitedly.

"That it's time to swap parts," Nick nodded and smiled.

"Mags could play the part of Kerry, the Irish lass we're shooting now. I'm sure Gabrielle won't mind playing Amanda, it's what she originally wanted anyway."

"We're in business then," Guy exclaimed and Margaret Anne could feel her heart pounding with sheer excitement.

"But this is wonderful," she said, looking from one of them to the other. "I can't believe that it's really happening to me."

Two days later the contracts were signed. Gordon, acting as her manager, had negotiated on her behalf and had hammered out a very satisfactory deal for her. In spite of his initial protestations, he was happy for her, especially since he could be on the spot and keep a close eye on her. There was still something about Nick Benson that unsettled him. The huge money was also a big consideration, one not to be frowned upon. Success was in the air.

CHAPTER 21

So it was that Margaret Anne Edwards reverted to her old name in fame -- Mags O'Dowd. Nick said she should definitely use her maiden name for the Irish connection, and that Mags was much more punchy and powerful than Margaret Anne. The Irish media were quick to learn of her starring role in an upcoming feature. After her first interview, in which her natural charm and humour shone through, the offers poured in. Mags O'Dowd was yet again a household name. The media loved her, and she basked in their ever- present attention, not to mention the prestige and notoriety that came with it. It was a dizzy merry-go-round of television and radio interviews as well as photographic sessions, and features for newspapers and magazines.

Her presence was in high demand at almost every social function, from judging beauty competitions to the local dog show. Mags O'Dowd was a big star shining brightly in the small firmament of her own native land, and she loved every moment of it.

Tonight however, as she lay in bed, with Gordon's strong arms encircling her, her thoughts were miles away. The little, small voice inside her gave her no peace and she couldn't sleep. You don't fall in love with a man like

Nick Benson, her voice kept saying to her. She sat up violently and lit a cigarette with shaking hands.

"Are you okay, baby?" Gordon asked tenderly, if a little drowsily.

"I'm fine, really I am, just restless that's all," she said, kissing him affectionately.

Should she confide in him, admit to him while they were here alone? After all Gordon and herself had a relationship unlike one she could have had with any other man. He never pried or asked questions, and she could ask him for any kind of advice, certain that he would give her an unprejudiced answer. She was so lucky really. You really shouldn't even like a man like Nick Benson. But she did.

It had happened after the first week of the picture when he had told her that her acting was superb and had complimented her on how quickly she had grasped the script. From then on her performances for him had become better and better as she began to feel a mad passion for this enormously talented and attractive man with his quiet, controlled charm and his strong, muscular body. They spent hours together going over technique. Her every performance was for him. She lit another cigarette and another as Gordon slept on peacefully beside her. It would be a mistake to tell him, she decided.

Maybe her feelings were purely professional. Maybe it was perfectly normal admiration for a man who could direct her as no one else could. This kind of admiration was perhaps often confused with love. Other actors had told her that you had to be a little in love with your director. And anyway directors were known to be highly seductive personalities. Otherwise they wouldn't be in the business they were in.

She could be excused for being only slightly in love, the little voice said, kinder to her now. But then if she were just infatuated, it should surely have stopped by now. The making of the film was over for months and her part had finished much earlier on.

Why did this have to happen to her? She was irritated now. This was the last thing she needed. He must have manipulated her in some way, pulled some physical strings, just the right words, the right looks. They were all the same, these film directors, hand-picked for the job. It was probably part of the game of making films. Damn him. What should she do?

She might have talked to Rose only Rose was so far up in the clouds at the prospect of her marriage to Jean Duvalle in a fortnight that it was impossible to bring her down to earth. She had gone to Paris to buy her trousseau and had actually stayed in Jean's luxury apartment in the Avenue Foch. Didn't she fall on her feet? Jean was coming to Kilbawn in the next day or two. A gigantic wedding was planned in the Catholic church, after which he was taking his new bride back to Provence to settle down in his villa to become the new Madame Duvalle. Even aside from that, Rose had become a total stranger to her in the last few months. Whether it was the fact that she was in love or perhaps a touch of the green-eyed monster on account of Margaret Anne's stardom, she didn't know. Regardless of the reason, Rose no longer seemed capable of treating Margaret Anne in the free and easy manner that had been so characteristic of her in the past.

The child in Margaret Anne's womb suddenly leapt, almost taking her breath away. She put her hands on her large stomach. Suddenly a little sigh of happiness trickled through her, and, as if by some divine intervention, she began to experience a lovely sense of contentment which totally banished the thoughts of her seductive director.

She looked lovingly at Gordon as he lay there, his blonde hair ruffled against the pillow. She knew then, without the shadow of doubt, that it was his real love, along with the baby she was carrying, that filled her with such abundant joyousness. Soon they would be three instead of two. She could hardly wait, she longed so for that moment to come. Eventually she put out her cigarette, turned off the bedside lamp, and lay down, the warm feeling of Gordon's body filling her with comfort and security. She closed her eyes and a wonderful sense of peace flooded her entire being.

Suddenly her father's face flashed vividly before her eyes and she realised that her memory of him was much sweeter and far less painful than it had ever been. Suddenly she knew that she no longer felt the need for the admiration and adulation of any other man. She was perfectly fulfilled and happy with her husband. You're out of my heart and my life now, Nick Benson, and I never again want to think of you.

"Thank you, God," she heard herself say from the very bottom of her heart. "Thank you that everything seems to be turning out so beautifully for me, and help me to stay like this."

And she knew at that moment that she had been healed and blessed.

CHAPTER 22

At exactly six-thirty the next morning, Gordon stepped out of the shower, dried himself, and put on his blue bathrobe. He walked over to the wash basin and, standing in front of the mirror, combed his damp, blonde hair and slapped on some aftershave. Then he quickly dressed and went into the bedroom to see Margaret Anne.

She was still fast asleep and he looked at her, at her beautiful serene face. He couldn't help thinking how lucky he was. The hotel was already showing a healthy profit, and the projections for the coming year were excellent. His wife had realised her dream and had become a star overnight. And the icing on the cake was the imminent birth of his baby. He leaned forward and kissed her lightly on the cheek without waking her. She'd been restless all night and hadn't dropped off until a few hours ago. He wondered what was on her mind. But, knowing Margaret Anne, if it were anything serious, she would tell him.

As he went to the dining room for breakfast he met Kieran in the foyer.

"Any news from abroad?" he asked brightly. "How is Madame Duvalle?"

Kieran smiled. "I had a phone call from the Bahamas," he replied. "She's in top form and sends her love."

"Well for some," Gordon remarked as he walked away.

Isn't it just? Kieran said to himself as he went through Reception and into his mother's office. His fiancee, Eithne Whelan, sat in his mother's place. Eithne was small and very pretty, her jet-black hair cut in pageboy style. But it was definitely her eyes that were her most striking feature. They were large, curiously elongated, almost, but not quite, almond-shaped, and as dark as pitch. Kieran went round the desk to her and gave her a little peck on the cheek.

"You look fabulous this morning, lemon suits you."

"That's what Dad says too," she replied. "You and he must have similar taste."

"Well you know what they say -- women always look for men who resemble their dads."

"And what about men?" she asked. "What sort of women do they look for?"

"Women just like you," he smiled.

"Pretty, sexy, and very good humoured."

Gordon strolled into the office a few minutes later.

"Good morning, you two," he greeted them affably, and led them to his own office for their usual, early-morning meeting. Lowering himself into the big swivel chair behind his desk, he said, "The most important item in today's agenda is the arranging of extra staff for the three functions this week."

"That's all in hand," Kieran replied, filling him in on the details.

"First class," Gordon said. "And presumably you have menus all agreed and in place," he said to Eithne.

"Yes, Mr Edwards," she said, showing him the arrangements for each of the functions.

"Do we have all this food in stock?"

"All except, of course, for the vegetables and the fish, which we'll get fresh on the day."

"How are the bookings?"

"No vacancies," Eithne was glad to report.

"Great stuff," Gordon exclaimed triumphantly.

"You better go get started, then."

Eithne smiled and left the office. Kieran then gave Gordon a list of the cheques he required, and, after careful scrutiny, Gordon signed them, muttering under his breath about the cost of everything. Just then the telephone on his desk rang and he picked it up.

"Oh, good morning, Mr O'Neill," Gordon said.

"We're ready to complete that bit of business. Everything seems to be in order now," the voice on the other end of the line said.

"That's absolutely fabulous," Gordon replied. "Do I need to call you later then?"

"Yes, say three o'clock this afternoon. And bring your cheque for the balance."

"Sure thing, thanks a lot," he said, hanging up.

He looked at Kieran, who was sitting there feeling awkward and uneasy.

"Guess what?" Gordon said. "I'm negotiating a wonderful surprise for Mags. I'll tell you about it later. In strictest confidence, you understand."

Then, looking at his watch, he sprang to his feet and left the office with an air of excitement. But a second later, as Kieran was rising to go, Gordon was back at the office door.

"Oh by the way, anything special in the post today?"

"Nothing of any great importance," Kieran said, "Mostly personal letters, charity requests, and the usual, daily stuff. I'll get it for you."

"You can drop it in to the apartment. I'll be there for the next hour or so. And remember, don't say a word about the surprise."

And he was gone again.

A moment later Gordon walked through the bedroom door. Margaret Anne, gazing out the window, did not hear him enter over the sounds of the television. She started in surprise when she felt his arms wrapping around her. Recovered, she looked lovingly up at him. He kissed her on the cheek.

"What are you doing at the window, love? You'll catch cold."

He had never seen her look more ravishing then she did this morning in her pink dressing gown. There was a peace and tranquillity in her expression that was almost ethereal. Pregnancy definitely suited her.

"I was thinking," she said softly.

"What about?" he asked, gazing into her eyes.

"Oh, everything that's happened in the last months. It's all like a dream, a beautiful dream, and sometimes I get the dreadful feeling that I'm going to wake up and find that none of it is true."

He held her very tightly.

"It's all very real, my love. And I am very happy for both of us."

"For the three of us," she corrected. "You musn't forget our baby."

She smiled and gently held her stomach in her hands. There was a gentle tap on the door.

"Who is it?" Gordon asked, remembering as he did so, that it would be Kieran bringing the mail.

"Anything exciting?" she asked, as he flicked through the pile of letters.

"This one's for you," he said, handing her a white envelope.

"Yippie," she shrieked in excitement.

"It's my first cheque from Phoenix Film Corporation."

To her surprise Gordon didn't respond. When she looked up at him she saw he was reading another letter. His face was as pale as death.

"What's the matter?" she asked, her joy suddenly turning to acute anxiety.

He didn't reply. In fact, he didn't appear to have heard a word she'd said as he stared at the letter in front of him.

In desperation she grabbed it from his hand and a photograph fell onto the floor. She snatched it up. Looking out from the photograph, straight at her, was a little, blonde boy of about five years who was the very miniature of Gordon. He was so like him that there could be no doubt. This was Gordon's son. She gasped in horror, feeling sick and faint from the shock. She threw herself on the bed and lay there on her side, her eyes filling with tears. She was unable to think clearly. Gordon, the bastard, had had a son and never told her.

Gordon walked to the window and stood there with his back to her, his hands dug deeply in his pockets. Damn you, Zoe, he repeated to himself, over and over again. You've screwed everything up now. Why, oh why, he asked himself, banging his fists against the window ledge in sheer frustration.

A few minutes ago he was about to clinch the deal on a huge surprise for Margaret Anne and now they had been hit with this terrific bombshell. This was the last thing he had expected to happen. The bolt from the blue that rightly hobbled him. He turned towards Margaret Anne. Why didn't she say something, ask him some questions, roar at him, hit him, anything but this dreadful silence?

He could stand it no longer. He walked across the room, turned off the television set, and sat on the edge of the bed. She curled her back to him, the letter clutched in her hand. She didn't move a muscle. He went around to the other side of the bed and kneeled in front of her.

"Mags," he said, "can we talk about this? I can explain, honestly I can."

"Who was she?"

"Her name was Zoe. We lived together."

"Why didn't you tell me?" she asked, shaking the photograph in his face.

"Because I didn't think it was important," he said, feeling like a guilty schoolboy.

"Not important?" she screamed, sitting up to face him.

The look in her eyes was so ferocious that it frightened him. There were tears in his eyes when he spoke again and his voice was suddenly husky and deep.

"Nothing is important to me but you, Mags. I couldn't compare you to Zoe Morgan. Mags, I love you, I never loved her. Please try to believe that. You are all that matters to me."

"Don't try to snow me," she shouted. "Why did you live with her if you didn't love her? And why didn't you have the decency to tell me?"

"Zoe nursed me when I was in a sanatorium coming down from a bad heroin trip. I was infatuated. She took care of me. I depended on her. We moved in together when I was emotionally on crutches. After four months we both realised it was a mistake, and we split by mutual agreement."

"Then where the hell did your son come from?"

"That's another story," he replied and hesitated, casting his eyes downwards, a look of concern on his face.

"Well, let's have it," she screamed. "Come on!"

"Well, Mags," he continued, pain in his eyes, "believe it or not I didn't even know I had a son until I read this letter. You see Zoe's married again, very happily, and she's led her husband to believe that the boy is actually his."

"She's some fast worker," Margaret Anne said sarcastically. "So why does she suddenly write to you now and send you a photograph of the son she's given another father? It doesn't make sense to me. And how did she know where to find you?"

"Brace yourself, this is going to be another shock. Nick Benson, your director, is her husband. He brought home some photographs with him. Now I know why he kept looking at me so strangely. Of course Zoe recognised me, and she got worried because Nick's been talking about coming back here for a holiday. With just her and the child. She wanted to put me on my guard."

Margaret Anne was stunned to silence. She had a queasy feeling in the pit of her stomach. Nick Benson. She repeated the name over and over again. It's crazy, all so very crazy. A myriad of thoughts and feelings again possessed her. Oh Nick, maybe she really was in love with him. Gordon reached out to her but she kept her distance. She was too confused.

Gordon noticed her extreme pallor and the faraway look in her eyes.

"Oh Mags, my dear Mags, don't be angry with me. I'm so sorry I didn't tell you about Zoe. But you were grappling with quite a few problems yourself, coming off drugs, the trauma with Jonathan Khan, your father's death. I didn't want to trouble you or upset you any further. Believe me I would have told you at some stage very soon."

She didn't hear a word he said. She was struggling fiercely again with her emotions. Who was this Zoe Morgan? Gordon's secret past with her suddenly took second place to Nick's present. What had this man done to her that she felt so bitterly disappointed? What an insane quirk of fate. Then the little voice inside her spoke again. I thought this was all over, you never again want to see this man, you love your husband very much. That's quite right, she replied to herself. How selfish of me. Poor Gordon must be heartbroken to know that Nick Benson is rearing his own son. She examined the photograph again. What a truly adorable boy. My poor Gordon.

She suddenly realised that Gordon was no longer in the room, and she filled with panic. She picked up the telephone beside the bed and dialled Reception. Eithne's voice was at the other end of the line.

"Eithne, tell Mr Edwards I need to speak to him, please."

"I'm afraid he's not on the premises at the moment."

Her heart pounded wildly now.

"Where has he gone?"

"I have no idea, Mrs Edwards. He drove off in a rush and he didn't tell anyone where he was going."

Margaret Anne banged down the phone with a mixture of temper and frustration. She threw herself back onto the bed, buried her head in the pillow, and cried bitter tears. She had never hated herself so much in all her life. An enormous sense of loss overwhelmed her and she was afraid, so very afraid. And she still couldn't help seeing the face of Nick Benson when she shut her eyes.

My God, my God, I've done it again. How terribly selfish of me. Poor Gordon. It's him I love. He must feel so upset and rejected wherever he is. How shocked and heartbroken he must be. Imagine hearing for the first time of his son's existence and then knowing that he was being raised by another man. How awful for him, how he must be hurting. And all I can think of is myself. She examined the photograph again and again as the tears streamed copiously down her cheeks. What an adorable boy he is, and what a wretch I am.

CHAPTER 23

As his silver Ford thundered along the wide open road, leaving the little village of Kilbawn and his wife further and further behind, Gordon clenched his teeth in anger. He was angry with himself for not having been open and above board with Margaret Anne, angry with Zoe for writing that ridiculous letter when she could have used the telephone, and angry with Margaret Anne because of her silent treatment, which had totally unnerved him. Damn her, why couldn't she understand? Wasn't her own past far more chequered? Despite that, didn't she know he loved her, and wasn't that all that mattered? If it were her he would have understood. He had been at her side when other men would have run a mile, and now he was cruelly shunned because of one secret which he never intended to keep anyway.

Then there was his son, his son, his own flesh and blood, who was being raised by another man. That had been a shock, and it hurt deeply. But there wasn't a thing he could do about it. There was no one he could even talk to about it. He felt lost and alone.

GOOD FOOD, GOOD DRINK, AND GOOD COMPANY was what the sign over the pub promised. Sounds good, Gordon thought. Why not? He stopped the car in the little car park at the side.

The atmosphere inside was warm and cheerful, full of happy people who didn't appear to have any problems.

"Double Scotch," he ordered and the bar man was quick to oblige. As the warmth of the whisky flowed through him, he relaxed somewhat. Things weren't that bad, after all. He ordered another Scotch and, drinking it, decided it was all just a storm in a teacup. It would sort itself out in time. He was making a mountain out of a molehill, he decided, having another drink and another. He felt as if the drinks had sharpened his befogged mind. He looked at his watch. It was two-fifteen, and he was due in Cork in the solicitor's office at three. He must look after that bit of business and forget all this other nonsense. He swallowed back his last drink and left with a spring in his step.

Pat O'Neill sat behind his large, old-fashioned, oak desk, studying Gordon, watching without comment as he signed the relevant documents. His hands trembled, and his breath gave off a very strong, repulsive smell of alcohol. Pat O'Neill was concerned for his client. This was definitely out of character with him. Puckering his eyebrows, he asked him quietly, "Is there something the matter, Gordon?"

"No, not at all, I'm great," Gordon retorted snappishly.

"That's not true, you know, you're not great," Pat O'Neill shot back.

"Oh for God's sake, I'm fine. Why do you ask, anyway?"

A curious smile appeared on the solicitor's face. Taking off his glasses, he said, "Well Gordon, I'm almost twice your age, and I am well and truly versed in the ways of the world. You've been drinking, rather a lot, and if I know you there is some reason for it."

"I'm celebrating, just celebrating. Am I not allowed that luxury?"

Pat O'Neill detected the irritation in his voice, so he decided to pry no further.

"Of course, Gordon, that's your own affair. Congratulations, anyway," he said, standing up and shaking him warmly by the hand.

"You've done an excellent piece of business, I can assure you of that."

Pat O'Neill walked with him to the door of the office and, noticing Gordon's unsteady gait, cautioned him.

"Why don't you take my advice, Gordon, and let me call you a cab? Or better still, I'll drive you home."

"No, not at all, there's no need. I'll be just fine," Gordon said as he left.

Ah well, Pat O'Neill thought, how can you save a man from himself?

"Time, gentlemen, please."

The barman's loud voice pounded through Gordon's head, which rested on the counter.

"Time for another drink," he slurred, raising his head with extreme difficulty.

"No more drink for you, sir. Come on now, it's almost midnight."

"I'm not going anywhere until I get another Scotch on the rocks."

At that juncture Gordon was lifted bodily and put outside the door. Several moments later he managed to work his way into the driver's seat of his car. He fumbled with the key in the ignition for a long time and then drove off.

He didn't notice the speedometer mounting as he pressed his foot harder and harder upon the accelerator. Nor did he hear the horns that wailed loudly as he sped along, ignoring traffic lights and failing to yield rights of way. Suddenly he felt strong, dazzling lights blinding his eyes. They became stronger and stronger as they neared. Then there was a loud crash, and then suddenly the lights were gone.

For what seemed like an eternity of desolate, disbelieving hours, Margaret Anne had wandered numbly about the apartment. She tried without success to pretend that at any moment she would hear Gordon coming down the stairs, hear his key in the lock, and see him enter the room. At regular intervals she phoned Reception, asking if he had returned, only to receive the same reply. In his absence she again began to take stock of herself, and she now realised how selfish she had been to the man who had done nothing but be good to her since the first day they'd met. She looked around the room, where they'd spent nearly all their evening hours for so long now, and saw the paintings he had bought her to cheer the place up, and the books, and the other little ornaments that he thought she would like. She thought of the loving moments they had shared, the patience and understanding he had always shown her, and she cried until there were no more tears left to shed. She knew now with absolute certainty that whatever her feelings for Nick Benson were, Gordon was the man she loved.

So it was with a face streaked with tears that she answered the telephone at three a.m. It was the night porter.

"Mrs Edwards?" he asked in a strange voice.

"Yes, Dave?"

"Sorry to disturb you, ma'am, but there is a Guard here at Reception, and he wishes to speak to you. He says it's urgent."

"Oh my God!" Margaret Anne sprang to her feet, alarm signals ringing through her head.

"I'll be right up," she exclaimed.

She trembled violently as she ran upstairs.

"Mrs Edwards?" the Guard asked, looking concerned and serious.

"That's right. Is there something wrong?"

"I'm afraid so," he replied quietly, seating her on a wicker armchair across the table from himself.

She knew instantly and burst into hysterical tears "It's Gordon, I knew it. Where is he? What's happened to him?"

"There's been an accident. He's at St Joseph's Hospital. I'm afraid he's seriously injured."

"What do you mean?" she demanded sharply.

"Just take it easy now, and don't be upsetting yourself too much in your condition. Can we call one of your own family, maybe your mother?"

"Oh no," she cried.

"She can't cope with anything. Take me to him please, right away."

As she rode with the Guard in the squad car, Margaret Anne quietly sobbed. Deep in her mind she willed Gordon to be all right. Every so often she burst into exclamations of self-condemnation.

"It's all my fault. I'm to blame. I drove him out because I was too stubborn and pig-headed to listen to him."

She could barely admit to herself that she'd been lost in thought about another man, but the knowledge of it made her feel even worse.

"There's no sense in blaming yourself," Garda Dunne tried to assure her. "Guilt and recriminations are one-way streets that lead nowhere except to misery and destruction. Try and be strong now and put on a brave front. Then you'll be a great help to yourself and to your husband."

"Mr Edwards is in emergency," the man at Reception informed her.

"Down the corridor and third door on the left."

A tall, slender, ginger-haired nurse met her at the door.

"You're his wife, I presume?"

Her grey-green eyes had a reassuring kindness in them.

"Yes. Is he going to be okay?" Margaret Anne asked urgently, her face anxious and full of questions.

Noticing her condition, the nurse was careful not to alarm Margaret Anne unduly.

"Well, he's unconscious at the moment, but we won't be able to tell the exact extent of his injuries until the doctors have finished their examination. In the meantime try not to worry. He's in very good hands, I can assure you."

"May I see him?"

"Not just yet," she said, leading her gently by the arm into an adjoining room.

"But when?" she asked fiercely, her blue eyes flaring.

"Very soon now. Can I get you a cup of coffee or tea perhaps?"

"Coffee would be nice, thank you."

As she sat there sipping the hot, soothing drink, her mind deeply engrossed in troubled thoughts, she kept seeing Gordon's face and the pain in his eyes as he tried to explain things to her. What if he didn't regain consciousness? Her mind balked at the idea. She couldn't bear even to contemplate it. I need him with me when I'm giving birth to our baby. I won't do it without him. She was overwhelmed with growing fear and anxiety.

After what seemed like an eternity, but was in reality only a little more than half an hour, the doctor entered the room. Margaret Anne jumped up immediately, staring sharply at him, searching his face for answers.

"Sit down, Mrs Edwards," he said, taking the seat opposite her.

Her heart pounded so furiously she thought that it actually might stop.

"Your husband has suffered what we call a closed head injury."

"What does that mean? Is it serious?" she interrupted.

"If you would let me finish please, Mrs Edwards, I will explain. It is a sudden injury to the brain, which occurred when he was thrown from the car at top speed. It's like a severe bruise which has caused fluid to accumulate. That's why he's unconscious. Obviously the sooner he regains consciousness the better, and we are doing everything possible to that end."

"How long do you think it will take?" she asked.

"It's hard to say, but the next forty-eight hours are crucial and will tell a lot."

"But what about the fluid, will it cause any permanent damage?"

"I don't expect so. When it disappears we can expect complete recovery. Meanwhile he has some facial lacerations and a broken arm, but thankfully no damage to the spine or pelvis."

"May I go to him now?" she asked with tear-filled eyes.

"Yes, but not for long. And afterwards I think you ought to go home and get some rest."

Smiling kindly, he shook hands with her and led her over to the reassuring, ginger-haired nurse. Margaret Anne walked nervously behind her into Gordon's room and seated herself in a comfortable armchair beside his bed. He lay there unconscious, various tubes and wires coming out of him, his body and head swathed in bandages. She rushed up to him and took hold of his limp hand.

Noticing Mrs Edwards's fearful expression, the nurse said, "There's no need to be afraid, pet, he's not really that bad. It might be a good idea to talk to him. He may even hear you. One never knows."

Margaret Anne's eyes lit up with hope.

"Do you really think so?" she asked.

"It's quite possible," the nurse replied.

"Anyway, I'll leave you alone with him for ten or fifteen minutes."

As Margaret Anne gazed at him, loving him with all her heart, not an eyelash flickered against his wan face. She brought her face close to his and kissed his cheek.

"I love you, Gordon," she whispered in his ear.

"Don't die, oh please don't leave me. Fight as hard as you can. I need you, we need you, the baby and I. There's not that much longer to go now. And I want you beside be when I am in labour, do you hear me? You promised you would, remember? I know you won't let me down. Can you hear me at all, Gordon?"

She stared at him for a long time, hoping and praying for even the most minute sign that he had heard. But there was none. He lay there so still, so very still. She ran her fingers through his blonde hair and then lay her head on his chest and sobbed until her body shook fiercely on his.

"I'm sorry, Gordon, so very sorry. Please forgive me. It was all my fault. I caused this terrible accident."

"Don't be so hard on yourself, my child," the voice said.

When she looked around she saw the Franciscan priest standing at the foot of the bed, looking at her with pity and love in his brown eyes.

"I'm Father Dominic," he said, coming towards her and giving her a very warm handshake.

"My name is Margaret Anne, Father, and that's my husband Gordon.

"On saying his name, she dissolved again into tears. The priest put his hand on her shoulder.

"May the good Lord comfort you," he said in a voice so loving and sincere that it touched a chord in her heart. She immediately felt a compelling urge to talk more to this man.

"Why should God comfort me?" she asked.

"Because he loves you very deeply, more than you could possibly comprehend."

"But Father," she continued, "I haven't practised my religion or even said a prayer since I was fifteen. I don't even know whether I believe in Him or not. I'm a pretty bad sinner, you know."

"We're all sinners, but he loves us just the same. Remember the prodigal son and the good shepherd?"

"Yes, I remember, but I wish I could really believe."

A thoughtful look crossed her face.

"The Bible never really made much sense to me. But if I thought that God would help me now, then I would believe."

"Then why don't you ask Him to help you and I know He will. He's loving and caring and concerned for every detail of your life."

"Okay Father, that's a deal," she replied.

"Let's pray together," he said.

Afterwards she felt a great peace.

"You know, Father," she said, "I believe there is something in what you say. Would you hear my confession?"

"Yes, to be sure," Father Dom said, filled with joy.

She knelt on the floor and told him everything, all of it, all the terrible, shameful, hurtful things she'd done in her short life. The priest did not blanch or scold. He looked down on her with love the whole while. When she finished Father Dom gave her absolution and blessed her.

"Oh, Father," she exclaimed, "I feel happier now. Thank you so much."

"Don't thank me, thank the good Lord who sought you out, using your husband's accident to bring you to him."

He then proceeded to anoint Gordon, and Margaret Anne joined with him wholeheartedly in the prayers. She didn't feel afraid any longer.

Father Dom noticed, however, how drawn and tired she looked.

"Let me drive you home now," he said.

"Gordon is in good hands, and you need your rest."

The next days seemed to take forever and Margaret Anne was at first impatient, nervous, and jumpy. But she found a solace she had never known before in her prayers.

Father Dom had given her a phone number at which she could reach him. She called him the next day. As it happened he was just here for a week visiting relatives in Cork. He had gone to the hospital solely to see if there were anyone there who needed comforting. He was always visiting the hospital, he explained, back home in Sacramento. Margaret Anne told him how she'd grown up nearby in San Diego. They spoke at great length, and Margaret Anne was amazed at the simple goodness this man exuded. She was heartbroken to hear that Dom would be leaving the next day. His family had spent all they could afford just to bring him over for this short time.

"Father Dom?" she asked at the end of the call.

"Yes?"

"If I were to bring my baby to Sacramento, would you perform the baptism? It would mean so much to me."

"It would be my privilege," he said and gave her his number and address. He promised he would pray for her and for Gordon and said goodbye. Margaret Anne hung up the phone and immediately began praying for Gordon as well.

At six o'clock three mornings later, she received the happy news that Gordon had regained consciousness and was asking for her.

She rushed to the hospital in a delirium of gratitude. Two weeks later, still weak, but gaining in strength by the day, Gordon was making a fine recovery at home, waiting in joyful anticipation for the birth of his baby.

CHAPTER 24

Gordon couldn't wait to give Margaret Anne the surprise of her life. He was getting impatient and frustrated, lying around recuperating with so much still to be done and so very little time to do it. He'd had to enlist Kieran to take care of the very special project for him because Margaret Anne insisted that he rest and obey the doctor's orders to the letter. And she watched him like a hawk.

"I'll never again take a chance on losing you," she had said to him lovingly, with tears in her eyes.

"You'll never know what I went through, looking at you lying there unconscious. It was awful but it made me realise how much I really loved you."

Gordon would always cherish those words in his heart. He knew now for certain that she really meant them.

Despite Gordon's anxieties, Kieran had assured him that everything would be completed in two days. Hopefully the baby wouldn't arrive before then. But he was sailing very close to the wind with just a week before Margaret Anne was due. He'd thought he might manage to escape out this afternoon while Margaret Anne was visiting the gynaecologist just to see for himself how everything was progressing. But on second thought he'd decided against it. He'd have to borrow a car for one thing. He still hadn't replaced the one totalled in the crash. He was sure to be caught out and it wasn't worth the risk.

He was stirred from his reverie by the sound of Margaret Anne's key turning in the door. He watched her as she ambled laboriously across the room. He couldn't help notice how beautiful she still looked, even with her now very rotund figure. There was something mature and mellow about her face, a softness and a peace. And the pale, blue maternity dress she wore accentuated her blue eyes.

"It's so warm," she said, throwing herself heavily on the couch beside him and kicking off her flat white shoes.

"Everything okay?" he asked holding her to him.

"We're both in ship shape," she replied, "but there's not a budge out of the baby yet. Dr Kearney reckons it will be at least another ten days."

Gordon breathed a sigh of relief. That gave him more than enough time.

"Let me fix you a cool drink," he said, going into the kitchen and returning in a few minutes with a large tumbler of orange juice laced with ice.

As she sat there sipping it to her heart's content, the telephone rang. She stretched across to the coffee table in front of her and picked it up.

"I'll be right there, Kieran," she said, her eyes suddenly alight.

"Where are you going?" Gordon asked immediately.

She smiled mysteriously.

"Come on, you come with me."

She caught his hand and led him to the door. Gordon was completely mystified.

"What's this all about? Where are we going?"

"Never mind now, just follow me."

He protested no further, and followed her blindly up the stairs, across the corridor, through the foyer, and down to the front door. A young man elegantly dressed in grey, flannel pants and dazzling white shirt stood outside in front of a gleaming, black Jaguar. He opened the rear door with a flourish.

"Step right in," he said and Margaret Anne led Gordon in ahead of her.

The young man started the car and it zoomed off. Gordon was dazed.

"What's this about?" he asked her.

"Is this a joke or something? Come on, Mags, where are you taking me?"

He was completely mesmerised, looking questioningly from Margaret Anne to the driver. Margaret Anne chuckled to herself throughout.

"Enjoy the ride now. Isn't she a beauty?"

He thought she was cracking up.

"Why couldn't we go for a ride in your car?"

"Relax, honey. I thought you would like to drive in style."

Gordon grew more intrigued by the minute. None of this was making any kind of sense to him.

Before he had an opportunity to ask any further questions the driver pulled up at Corrigan's Garage. He smartly stepped out of the car, opened the back door, and handed the key to Gordon.

"Congratulations, Mr Edwards," he said. "You are the proud owner of a brand new Jaguar Coupé."

Gordon was speechless. As he took the key, he sat there immobilised with excitement and confusion for several seconds. Then he looked at his wife in sheer wonder. She threw her arms around him.

"It's my way of saying I love you and welcome home," she said.

"Oh, Mags, this is too much. You shouldn't have, really you shouldn't --"

Then, noticing a slightly disappointed look start to enter her face he added, "But thanks my love. She's a gem. You're one in a million, Mags."

He was touched almost to the point of tears.

"This must have set you back quite a lot," he continued rather seriously when he'd composed himself.

"Not really," she replied. "Let's just say my film cheque almost covered it."

"I have a surprise for you also," he announced as he drove the smooth, beautifully-handling car home.

"You have?" she replied. "When do I get to see it?"

"Soon now, very soon. And that's all I'm telling you."

It was to be sooner than he had thought. On their way in, Kieran beckoned to Gordon from Reception.

"Excuse me a second, Mags," he said.

As Gordon went towards him, Kieran handed him an envelope and whispered, "This is the message. Everything is ready, and I think it's only magnificent."

"Thanks a lot, Kieran."

He winked knowingly and rejoined Margaret Anne.

"What did Kieran want?" she asked.

Gordon found himself at a loss -- he hadn't expected the question. Boy, but she noticed everything.

"Just a little business matter he was taking care of for me, nothing important," he replied casually before changing the subject.

"Shall we have dinner in the apartment tonight?"

"Yes, I think that would be nice and cosy. Besides I can hardly climb the stairs anymore."

"You poor kid," he remarked benevolently.

"It won't be long more now, I hope."

Inside the apartment, Margaret Anne flopped onto the bed and pushed herself into a pile of pillows, trying to find a comfortable position. She felt awkward and ungainly, her feet slightly swollen all of a sudden.

"Are you okay," Gordon asked, noticing her pained expression. "Is it the baby?"

"No such luck. I'm fine, really, it's just that I'm a bit stiff today.I wish this baby would come, though. I feel so huge."

After dinner, as Margaret Anne sat on the bed, sipping steaming coffee out of a long, delicate, white mug, she noticed that Gordon's eyes were dancing mischievously as he came towards her.

"What's with you?" she asked, eying him curiously.

"Nothing escapes you, Mags O'Dowd-Edwards, does it?"

She smiled radiantly at this.

"Well, if you must know," he continued, "I'm feeling very pleased with myself."

"Good for you," she exclaimed. "And what's brought this on?"

"You'll know tomorrow when I take you for a little drive and show you something."

She sat up on the bed, alive with curiosity.

"This sounds very mysterious. I can't imagine what it's going to be."

"Don't tax your pretty little brain," he replied. "You would never guess."

CHAPTER 25

In the morning as Margaret Anne eased her now aching body out of bed, she suddenly remembered her last conversation with Gordon. Immediately, she felt almost nimble. Just thinking about the surprise made her smile and she could think of nothing else as she threw on her housecoat and went into the kitchen where the coffee was already brewing. The smile was still dancing in her eyes when Gordon emerged from the shower, his blonde hair dripping onto his white bathrobe.

"Someone is up bright and early," he remarked, coming towards her and embracing her.

"Someone is really looking forward to her mystery tour," she chuckled excitedly.

Her mind raced, trying to imagine what it possibly could be.

Gordon read her like a book.

"I've already told you that you'd never guess," he said cavalierly, enjoying himself.

After a few moments she suddenly announced confidently, "I have it, it's a pony for the baby."

"A very good idea, but wrong," he retorted, amused but also relieved.

He couldn't bear it if she guessed correctly. And knowing her, she was just sharp enough to do it. It was time to go.

And so on this fine morning, with the sun shining brilliantly from a cloudless, Asia-blue sky, Gordon eased his new car out of the tall, iron gates of the hotel, and turned left up a narrow hill. Margaret Anne rolled down the window and took a deep breath in an effort to quell the excitement that raged inside her and made her heart beat rapidly. She took off her sunglasses to get a clearer view of her surroundings and, of course, in the hope that she would find some clue that would point to their unknown destination.

"There's nowhere like the seaside when the weather is beautiful, nowhere in the wide world," she remarked.

"I prefer it in winter when the white horses are heaving over the water and lashing against the rocks. There's something awesome and thoughtful about it. Just like my wife when she has a tantrum."

Gordon glanced out of the corner of his eye to gauge her reaction. She was smiling to herself.

"You flatter me," she replied. "And I won't forget to bring that statement to your mind the next time I flare up."

She hit Gordon playfully on the arm and then leaned back in the seat. She was just relaxing when she felt the car slowing down. She sat up immediately, peering curiously through the window, her eyes swiftly scanning the scene that confronted her.

Gordon got out of the car, opened the timber gate of a bungalow, sat back into the car, and drove up the little curving drive to the front door. She didn't utter a syllable but just waited with bated breath in the passenger seat as he got out again, walked up to the door, and rang the bell, careful to keep his back to her as he did so.

The door opened slowly and Margaret Anne gasped in astonishment when she saw her mother standing there looking radiant in a floral, cotton sundress. Fancy Mum coming to live here right beside us. What a really beautiful surprise, she thought to herself as she struggled awkwardly out of the car. Grainne came out to help her, followed by Gordon, with a happy, smiling face that was now flushed with excitement.

"Oh mum, this is only wonderful," Margaret Anne exclaimed, hugging her warmly.

"I am so happy, so very happy. I can't believe it."

She then looked to Gordon.

"You sure were right. I never would have guessed this."

Grainne was overcome, and with tear-filled eyes she said, "I've never seen you look more beautiful than you do today. Pregnancy definitely suits you."

"I'm afraid I feel anything but beautiful at the moment," she replied, looking down at her large stomach and envying her mother's slim figure.

She felt more monstrous than ever. Gordon grew impatient.

"Aren't you going to show us around?" he asked Grainne.

"Of course, come along."

She led them through the sliding porch door and then through the oak front door with its brass knobs and knockers. The hall was bright and spacious, decorated in a pretty shade of mimosa with a highly polished oak floor. A magnificent, Persian rug rested in its centre. The first door on the right led onto a very large, sun-drenched lounge, furnished with a simple, yet distinctive, elegance. Charming, mahogany tables, built-in presses and whatnots were mingled with comfortable armchairs, and a vast, white, leather sofa took pride of place. The walls were tastefully decorated in a smooth, pastel lavender and graced by several, carefully-chosen pictures which blended perfectly with the tone and mood of this lovely room. Margaret Anne was totally lost in wonder and admiration at the beauty of it all.

As she was led across the hall into the dining room she exclaimed, "This is only just divine. It gets more beautiful as we go."

"I call this the oak room," her mother announced, and Margaret Anne noticed her wink at Gordon.

"I must congratulate you Mum, you sure have done an excellent job," she said, admiring the huge, oak table and chairs and the oak bookcase in the corner. Even the pictures on the walls of this room had oak frames which contrasted well with the cool, cream decor.

Moving in and out of the bedrooms, Margaret Anne was flabbergasted at the perfection of it all. The soft, integrated tones of colour everywhere were in perfect harmony with the carpets and curtains. She couldn't help thinking of how nice it would be if she and Gordon had a home just like this. The master bedroom, with its air of warmth and comfort, held a very special appeal for her.

Looking at the large double bed, her mind posed some very pertinent questions.

"You must be planning a second marriage, Mum," she remarked jovially, but very much in earnest.

"You could never tell," her mother replied.

"I'm hardly on the scrap heap yet."

"Whoever he is," Gordon interjected, "he's a very lucky guy. And I guess he'll have nothing to do but hang up his hat."

"The best of luck to him," Margaret Anne said wistfully. "But he'd want a lot of class to compare with Dad."

Grainne was anxious to change the subject. She didn't like the tone of her daughter's last remark and she wouldn't want anything to cast a cloud on this very special occasion.

"I'm dying for a cup of tea," she said, heading straight for the kitchen.

As she crossed the threshold of this bright, cheerful, red-and-white room, Margaret Anne sucked in her breath with sheer excitement. There in the centre of the round, red table was a huge cake which was an exact replica of the bungalow. She was speechless as she read the icing writing on the roof: "Home sweet home. To Mags with love".

She looked wide-eyed and open-mouthed from Gordon to her mother and then to the cake until the full realisation finally struck her. She was pale and trembling with excitement and delight.

"You don't mean that this bungalow is really ours?" she said, looking directly at Gordon.

"Every square inch of it," he replied.

"I do hope you like it."

She fell into his arms, words of love and gratitude pouring out of her.

"Oh Gordon I love you," she gasped again and again. "Thank you, oh thank you. It is so beautiful."

Then she turned to her mother, who was standing there looking very pleased and happy for her daughter.

"Oh mum," she cried, embracing her.

"Isn't it absolutely marvellous? I would never have guessed."

"I'm delighted for you, Margaret Anne. And I'm sorry Dad isn't here to see it. But somehow I feel he's watching us from heaven."

There were tears in Grainne's eyes as she spoke, but, despite them, she was truly happy.

"You acted your part very well," Margaret Anne added and Gordon agreed wholeheartedly.

"We had it all well planned and rehearsed, your mother and I. And she carried it through like a dream."

As they sat at the table drinking tea from the tall, red-and-white mugs, Margaret Anne became suddenly serious and pensive.

Gordon was quick to notice the change of mood.

"What's going on in that brain of yours now, my love?" he enquired tenderly.

"Well, I was just thinking of what all this cost and I was wondering how you managed to pay for it. I presume you got a mortgage?"

"You presume wrong. I didn't borrow a single dime."

Margaret Anne was puzzled and intrigued now.

"I didn't think you had this kind of money."

"Well, I've had some stocks and shares for many years, and three months ago they took a huge leap, spiralling right up to heights that I had never dreamt. I struck while the iron was hot, cashed them in, and made a very handsome killing."

"Wow, that was lucky. And where did you get the time to furnish and decorate it so beautifully?"

"Kieran took care of that for me. With great help from your mother, I might add. Not to mention a couple of ideas from myself thrown in."

"I can hardly believe it, it's all so wonderful. I will never forget this day, and I'll tell my children all about it, every detail of it. What a lovely story for them, a true fairy tale."

"Speaking of children," Gordon continued, rising from his seat, "we have something else to show you, something we had to keep until the very end, otherwise it would have been a give away."

"But what more could there possibly be?" she asked as Gordon led her to a door beside the master bedroom.

Grainne handed him a key.

"You didn't see this," he said, his eyes sparkling with delight as he opened the door.

Margaret Anne beamed with pleasure and looked in wonder around this room. It was decorated mainly in a cheerful combination of lemon and white with dashes of pink and blue here and there. Large nursery rhyme prints covered the walls and little, multi-coloured lamps.were spread about It was a veritable delight, she thought, lovingly touching the white cradle, the big rocking horse, and the large, cuddly toys. She felt a joy and happiness she had never experienced before.

"You thought of everything," she said softly and with heartfelt appreciation.

She ran to Gordon and Grainne and kissed them both.

"Everything is ready for the birth of our baby now," he said. "Our part is done. Over to you now, Mags. Time for you to do your work."

Later that evening as they drove home, Margaret Anne thought over this most extraordinary day.

"How could I have ever doubted?" she thought aloud.

Arching his brows, Gordon looked over at her.

"Did I hear you mutter something about doubt?"

She hadn't intended her remark for his ears, and she hesitated in silence for a moment. Then, plucking up her courage, she decided to tell him.

"You know, Gordon," she began, "I actually thought I had fallen in love with Nick Benson. I mean I was definitely infatuated with him, of that there is no doubt. But when you told me Zoe was married to him, I think I actually felt jealous. I know now, of course, how wrong I was. And I feel so guilty and ashamed. I do love you very much, Gordon, and I'm grateful for your love and care and concern for me. And especially for this magnificent gift you've given us. My God, Gordon, you have been so good to me. I really don't deserve you."

Gordon took his left hand from the steering wheel and held hers tightly.

"I will always love and cherish you, Mags. Let's put the past behind us now. I understand well how you felt about Nick Benson, because, as I've already explained to you, I had a similar experience with Zoe when she nursed me. The only difference was I acted impulsively and moved in with her."

She leaned her head lovingly on his shoulder.

"The Lord has certainly blessed me with the best husband in the world, and I will always thank Him for that."

Gordon stared ahead, a sort of quizzical smile on his face. Did she say the Lord? His wife was definitely changing out of all proportion. He made no comment for a few moments.

"A penny for your thoughts," she said.

"They're worth a great deal more, you'll have to up the price."

"Come on, Gordon," she begged, "you're making me curious now."

"Okay, Mags," he continued, "I've just been thinking about how religious you've become lately. I remember a time not so long ago when you didn't even believe in God. Remember how your mother's little, red Sacred Heart lamp used to irritate you?"

"Yes, I remember. But that's all changed now. I met a saintly Franciscan priest who gave you the last rights when you were in hospital. I made my confession to him."

Gordon was astounded. This was one of the biggest surprises he'd ever received.

"I'll have to hand it to that holy man, God bless him. He must have frightened the living daylights out of you."

"You should know me better than that by now. No one coerces or scares me. But Father Dominic seemed to say just the right things. And you know, I don't know how to explain it, but while he was talking to me I felt my heart soften. And I had this compelling urge to make my peace with God. He made me feel good."

She was silent for a few minutes with a faraway look in her eyes.

Then she announced, "I'm going to ask him to baptise the baby and if it's a boy, I'll definitely call him Dominic."

"That's nice, and if it's a girl?"

"I like Kim. What do you think?"

"Short and sweet, it would suit perfectly. Kim Edwards, yes there is a nice ring to that."

CHAPTER 26

At three-fifteen the next day, Margaret Anne was in St Joseph's hospital, in the throes of labour. Gordon, dressed in full hospital regalia, including white coat, hat, and mask, stood beside her. He held her hand tightly and encouraged her along with kind, loving words, keeping her spirit up with cheerful chatter in the intervals between contractions. If the truth were really known, he didn't feel so hectic himself. He swore he could almost feel the terrible pain she was suffering every time she moaned in agony.

Dr Kearney came in at six o'clock, and, after a careful examination, he spoke to Gordon who'd waited outside the door.

"Everything seems to be normal, but I'm afraid there is a long day and night ahead of you. Your baby won't be born until after sundown, I would think."

"That's a long time," Gordon replied, concern written all over his face. "Is there anything you could give her to help her on?"

"Yes, I have instructed Nurse O'Brien to connect a drip, and I'll be back a little later on in the night."

"Thank you, Doctor," he said, before returning to his wife's bedside, nervous now at the prospect of the long hours ahead. It was an arduous, wearying, exhausting struggle. And it went on and on as Margaret Anne writhed in pain, her hair wet and dishevelled. Gordon's heart ached for her. He felt so helpless and frustrated that he grew impatient with the nurse, who seemed to be showing very little concern for Margaret Anne.

"My God, can't you do anything for her?" he protested. "Surely there must be some easier way."

"It's up to herself. She'll have to make a greater effort," came the cold reply.

Gordon's nerves were frayed and he was taut and irritable. He glanced at his watch. It was approaching ten o'clock.

"I want the doctor here, right away," he ordered, "I'm not happy with the treatment my wife is receiving."

"Mr Edwards," the nurse cautioned him quietly, "if you can not keep calm, you are no help, and you'd be better off to go home."

Gordon was infuriated at this.

"Go home? Be calm? How can a man be calm while he's watching his wife in acute agony, with no medical treatment? I insist that you call the doctor," he repeated angrily.

"It's his duty to be here and I don't intend to stand idly by and watch my wife suffer one minute longer."

Dr Kearney came through the door soon afterwards.

"Having a bad time?" he smiled at Margaret Anne.

She could barely answer him. He seemed to be monitoring the baby's heartbeat at very regular intervals and Gordon noticed an anxious expression appear on his face. The doctor then beckoned Nurse O'Brien to come with him into the office. While they were away every minute seemed like an hour until finally Nurse O'Brien popped her head through the door.

"Could you come outside for a moment?" she asked and, as Gordon approached her, she continued.

"Dr Kearney would like to have a word with you."

"There's something wrong, isn't there?" he asked, panic and fear in his eyes.

"Please, Mr Edwards," she replied coldly, "try to get a grip on yourself."

She then led him into the office where Dr Kearney was standing at the desk.

"Sit down, Mr Edwards," he said. Gordon sat uneasily on the edge of the chair.

"Now," he began, "your wife is having difficulty bringing the baby into the world because the birth is in breach. You see, we are unable to turn the baby at this stage. Right now the child is in distress and the heartbeat is weakening."

Gordon's heart pounded and his legs became weak.

"My God, Doctor, can you do anything about it?"

"I'm afraid I'll have to perform a Caesarian section immediately. With your consent of course."

"Is there any danger to my wife?"

"None that we can foresee, but then, as in any other operation, one never knows."

"I suppose you'd better go ahead if it means saving the baby."

At eleven-thirty, Dr Kearney performed a Caesarian section on Margaret Anne. The child she delivered was perfect, but the mother was weak and still very heavily sedated. Dr Kearney brought the news to Gordon who had been waiting in another room for over two hours while the operation lasted. He had paced the floor for most of that time, his thoughts and heart with Margaret Anne in the theatre. He couldn't forget her face steeped in pain and how she'd clutched at him in desperation like a drowning person. There had been something so helpless and so very pathetic about her. The memory of it all had brought tears to his eyes. The door opened and Dr Kearney came in.

"You have a baby girl, Mr Edwards," he announced without prelude. Gordon spun around to face the Doctor. "Is my wife okay?"

"Yes, she's fine, but very weak at the moment. And of course she will be sore for a few days. She's sleeping now and we'll keep her sedated for a further twelve hours. Now, about your daughter, she's perfect, a little beauty. She weighs six pounds, ten ounces."

Gordon grasped the doctor's hand.

"Thanks very much, Doctor. I'm so relieved that they're both all right. When can I see them?"

"Well, you can look in on your wife in about an hour, but you can see your daughter right away."

They left the room together and walked down the corridor to the ante-natal nursery where new babies were taken immediately following their birth. A nurse lifted the baby from the cot and brought her over to the window for him to see. Gordon was highly emotional as he looked in wonder at his very own daughter.

"She's beautiful, a darling baby," he whispered, his eyes lit. "I wish Mags could see her."

"Perhaps tomorrow, all going well," the doctor replied.

A DAUGHTER FOR MAGS O'DOWD-EDWARDS was how the morning paper, in bold, black, print, heralded the birth of Kim Edwards. In its wake all hell broke loose. Newspaper and magazine reporters, along with media people from radio and television, bombarded the hospital, all eager to interview Margaret Anne and to get photographs of mother and baby. Because of her weak condition the hospital staff adamantly refused them admission. The media persevered undaunted in their efforts until it became necessary to transfer her secretly to another room. As soon as she was well enough, however, the media had their way and the saga of Mags and Kim was the talk of the land.

"You're a little star in your own right already," Gordon said to his baby daughter as he lay her in her cot after one of these photographic sessions.

Margaret Anne's room at the hospital was like a garden in full bloom with bouquets, pots, and baskets of flowers everywhere. She was extremely touched by the number of cards and letters she received from her fans. Gordon never realised there were so many of them out there.

"Isn't it heartening to think of the thought behind each of these cards?" she remarked to him, looking at the vast array.

"They all love you, Mags," he replied. "I guess I'll have to learn to share you with them." He suddenly remembered something, and, putting his hand into the inside pocket of his jacket, he produced another letter.

"Speaking of mail," he said, "this one arrived this morning. It's from America."

"Don't tell me the news has travelled that far already," she exclaimed as she tore it open and began to read. He noticed her blush before she looked up and told him what it was.

"It's from Nick Benson. It's an invitation to the premiere of the film at the Cannes Film Festival," she said, bubbling over with excitement.

"What a lovely surprise When is it?"

"Next May," she replied. "Kim will be almost a year old then and we'll be able to bring her along with us. I can't wait to show her off."

"The proud mother already," Gordon remarked with a smile. "And with every reason, I might add."

"You always say the right things, that's what I love about you."

She kissed him lovingly. He thought she looked radiant. Her eyes were sparkling.

"Oh, Gordon, it'll be great to see the film. Isn't it something to look forward to? I hope I'll have my figure back by then."

"Vanity, thy name is woman," he retorted and then a thought suddenly struck him.

"Wouldn't it be nice to visit Rose while we're in France? I'm sure she'd love to see Kim. Let's make it a real vacation. You deserve it."

"Yes," she replied, "that would be nice -- our first family vacation. And I say you deserve it, Gordon Edwards."

A week later Margaret Anne and Kim were home with Gordon in the bungalow. As they lay in bed together that first night home, Gordon took her in his arms.

"It's great to have you back again, love, I really missed you."

"Me too," she replied, relaxed and happy in his strong embrace.

"Do you think Kim will sleep all night?" he asked.

"Not a chance, she's due a feed at two a.m. and another at six."

"I'll take care of that," Gordon said. "You need your rest."

Margaret Anne suddenly sat bolt upright in the bed.

"You know what I was thinking?"

Startled, Gordon responded, "I have no idea but I sure would like to know."

"We must go ahead and make the arrangements to bring Father Dominic over here for the Christening. It would mean such a lot to me. I owe that priest a great deal. I believe he's a saint. Do you think we could do it?"

"No reason why not," Gordon assured her. "We can afford it and if it makes you happy it'll be worth every cent. I'll make the necessary arrangements with the travel agent."

"Oh thank you, Gordon, I'll ring him tomorrow and see if he can make it."

Father Dominic arrived at Shannon Airport ten days later. Margaret Anne had been anxiously awaiting the touchdown of the jumbo jet which was forty minutes late. When finally she saw him emerge through the passenger door her heart leapt for joy and she ran towards him, greeting him with a warm hug.

"Thank God you got here. It's really wonderful to see you again. I'm so happy."

He smiled at her with an expression of love and gratitude, but she thought he looked tired and worn as well.

"You've given me the treat of my life and I thank you from the bottom of my heart," he replied.

Father Dom spent a week with them at The Harbour Star and in that short space of time he endeared himself to all, hotel staff and villagers alike.

"That man's a saint, if ever I met one," Mick the Mouth was heard to say, and Bobby Twomey began to go to Mass again after twenty-five years.

Kim's Christening was a most touching ceremony and Margaret Anne never forgot the words Father Dominic said afterwards.

"She's a little angel now. Let's pray that she will always remain as she is tonight, and that she will go through this vile world without being tarnished by it."

"Your blessing and prayers have given her a pretty good start. I believe you have great influence with the man above."

"Not one bit more than yourself. The Lord has done wonderful things for you. Keep Kim safe for him."

Afterwards Gordon drove Father Dom to his relatives and Margaret Anne and Kim came along also. He spent two weeks there with his brother and sister, and, at the end of that time, they said a fond goodbye to him as he left from Shannon to return to his children in Sacramento.

PART THREE -- FRANCE

CHAPTER 27

A letter from Ireland, Rose thought happily, as she tore open the envelope. The photograph was the first thing she saw and she gasped with admiration. Little Kim six months old, how time flies. Isn't she beautiful? A little darling. How lucky Gordon and Margaret Anne are. Wouldn't she just love a little daughter like that? But sure, she was a bit past her prime now. She went out to the terrace where Jean sat, sheltered from the blazing Mediterranean sun by a large, colourful umbrella.

"Isn't she just adorable?" she gushed, handing him the photograph. He put his newspaper on the table in front of him and studied the picture closely.

"Une belle enfant certainement, just like her mother."

"I think she's more like Gordon," she said, taking back the picture and studying it further. "Undoubtedly she has her mother's big, blue eyes, but her general expression, that is definitely her father's, so soft and sensitive."

Jean poured Rose a cup of coffee and she sat opposite him, looking dreamily out at the deep, blue sea and the hazy mountains rising majestically behind it. She suddenly remembered the letter. She had become so enraptured by Kim that she'd forgotten to read it. As she did so, her eyes lit up with excitement.

"Oh Jean, they're coming here to stay with us for two weeks on their way to the Cannes Film Festival. They'll be with us in ten days time. Isn't that wonderful? I just can't wait."

"I am so pleased for you ma chère. We will show them a good time, and make their vacation memorable," he promised, taking hold of her hand and squeezing it affectionately.

Margaret Anne and Gordon decided to travel by car. They preferred the freedom and convenience of it, especially with all the knick-knacks one has to bring along with a baby. They travelled to Cork, set sail for Roscoff, and then made their way leisurely south along the motorway, down the Autoroute du Soleil. They took three days to complete the trip. Margaret Anne enjoyed every moment of it, and even little Kim, seated in state in the baby seat in back, seemed aglow with joie de vivre as she cooed and gurgled and kicked her bare feet with excitement.

"Here we are," Gordon announced as he drove into the beautiful city of Avignon, with its large fountains, monuments, and lively bistros. Gordon stopped the car at the bridge and they got out singing merrily "sur le pont d'Avignon" as they looked into the waters of the Rhone.

"It's great to be alive," Margaret Anne exclaimed, hugging Kim with one hand and Gordon with the other.

"It's absolutely heavenly," Gordon replied. "Wouldn't it be lovely to have a photograph of the three of us taken right here?"

"Yes, it would be lovely, but not possible I'm afraid."

"Maybe not," Gordon said, "but we might get lucky."

He then walked towards a tall, slender, middle-aged gentleman who was approaching just at that moment.

"Parlez vous Anglais?" Gordon asked in his American tone.

"Yes," came the welcome reply and the kindly gentleman did the needful.

Back in the car again, they began to study Rose's instructions about the meeting place. Over the bridge, it read, onto the Autoroute again, and off at the third outlet. Drive on a narrow, tree-lined road for about twenty eight kilometres, and you will see a pretty, yellow café on your right with a huge sign reading Chez Bertrand. They were to phone from there and Rose would be along in about twenty minutes.

They were sitting out in front of the café, drinking cool, white wine and enjoying the warm Mediterranean sunshine, when the white Renault came to a halt. Rose alighted, looking radiant in a pale, green, cotton sundress which accentuated her beautiful, bronzed skin.

"Thank God, you're here at last," she said and embraced them warmly.

"I was really expecting you yesterday, and I was getting worried. I've been longing so much for your visit."

"I guess we took our time driving down," Gordon replied. "It was so hot we needed a break every so often."

"You look fantastic, just blooming," Margaret Anne remarked. "This climate certainly suits you."

"Oh, it's perfectly beautiful here, I just adore it. I can't imagine how I ever survived for so long in the damp climate at home."

"Here's someone who seems to thrive quite well in it," Gordon announced, lifting Kim from the carry cot which lay in the grass in the shade of a spreading tree.

There were tears in Rose's eyes as she took her in her arms.

"You beautiful baby," she exclaimed, hugging and kissing her. "What a wonderful little traveller."

The proud parents looked at each other lovingly, and Gordon gave his wife a little peck on the cheek. They drove behind Rose for about a further ten kilometres until her indicator flashed to the left. They followed her through a large, ornamental gate and up a curving driveway. Their route was bordered by pines and spacious green lawns that swept down from the terrace past a glittering blue swimming pool. The house was tall and gracious, its exterior walls painted a soft yellow, so pale that it looked sandy. The timber shutters shading the windows were of a deeper shade of the same colour. The inviting wide terrace, with its balustrade of white stone and marble, stretched along the front of the house with a panoramic view of the glittering blue sea.

Jean waited there to greet them, looking twenty years younger than his age, in khaki shorts and yellow t-shirt.

"You are all very welcome," he said, kissing them warmly on both cheeks.

"Thank you so much," Gordon and Margaret Anne replied in one voice.

"You sure have a heavenly spot here," Gordon continued. "You're a lucky woman, Rose."

Jean beamed proudly now as he turned to his wife.

"Well, my Rose, what do you say to that?"

"Oh yes, to be sure I am," she replied. "But aren't you lucky to have me here with you?"

"Oui, oui, but of course, my love. How often have I told you so?"

He paused and looked from Gordon to Margaret Anne, gesticulating frantically as he continued, "My Rose has made me feel young again, jeune, très jeune."

"And you certainly look it," Margaret Anne commented, rather embarrassed by his amorous excess.

"Enough of that now," Rose said, anxious to get her guests settled in.

"Come inside. I'm sure you're dying to see your room, and to freshen up before dinner. We eat at seven sharp so you've got four hours to yourselves."

Inside, the cool, lofty rooms were filled with lovely, filtered sunlight. They were elegantly furnished. The floors were of highly polished parquet, and covered here and there with large, Persian rugs. Throughout the house colours were pale and cool, with cream and white predominating. The same colours were repeated in the fabrics that hung on the windows and covered sofas and chairs. The whole house seemed to exude a warm, welcoming atmosphere.

Inside their airy bedroom Gordon and Margaret Anne couldn't resist the large, inviting, four-poster bed. As they looked at Kim fast asleep in the sturdy, oak cot, they decided to do likewise. It was the chime of the ornamental clock hanging on the wall that woke them up abruptly. They both started in surprise and glanced across at it.

"My God, it's six-thirty already," Margaret Anne said. "We'll never be ready for dinner."

"We'll make it, let's go," Gordon said, and Margaret Anne was on her feet and into the shower.

They dined in style in the enchanting dining room with its long bleached oak table. Jean presided at the top, with Rose on his right. The food was delicious, cooked by their invaluable housekeeper, René, who'd been trained in a large, Parisian hotel. First came consomme with a beautiful, wild flavour, followed by a scrumptious paté with mushroom provençale, and then roast lamb with sauté potatoes, broccoli, and creamed carrots. And the orange soufflé provided a very soothing finish to the delectable meal.

"I must get a few nice recipes from René for the hotel," Margaret Anne said. "It's so hard at times to vary the menus."

"Yes," Rose replied, "I used to have the same difficulty. By the way, how is the hotel doing, still as well as ever I presume?"

"It's going a bomb, a real goldmine, we sure were very lucky," Margaret Anne said.

"Of course Kieran and Eithne are doing a great job," Gordon said. "You did hear that they are planning to marry at Christmas?"

"Oh yes, I'm delighted. Eithne is a darling," Rose said.

"And Kieran is so like my Rose," Jean interjected. "I feel for him like my own son."

"We're giving them our little apartment downstairs just until they get on their feet," Gordon said.

"That'll be lovely for them, so convenient," Rose replied.

Some minutes later Jean changed the subject.

"So you're off to Cannes for the film festival?"

"That's right, we leave in ten day's time."

Gordon looked with pride at his wife.

"They're showing the premiere of Fresh Pastures, so I guess Mags is hitting the high spots."

"Is it in competition?" Jean asked.

"No, but the Phoenix Film Company are hoping to sell the rights for a large profit."

"Speaking of Cannes," Rose interrupted, addressing Gordon and Margaret Anne, "I was wondering if you would do a little favour for me."

Jean was curious now. What could his wife possibly want that he couldn't give to her?

"Sure, if we can," they replied in unison, wondering what on earth she was going to ask.

Rose smiled coyly now as she continued.

"I would really love to keep Kim here with me while you're away, just a loan of her. It would make me so very happy, and I'm sure it would be far better for her also. And of course it would leave you two completely free."

Gordon and Margaret Anne looked from one to the other. It was Margaret Anne who spoke first.

"I guess we could live without her for two weeks."

Gordon nodded in full agreement.

Jean looked quizzically at his wife, his face slightly flushed. Was this her way of telling him that she was lonely or that she would love a child of her own? His musings were interrupted by Henri, the house boy.

"Monsieur Edwards, pour le téléphone," he said to Jean.

"It's a telephone call for you, Gordon, you can take it in the morning room. Henri will take you there."

"That's strange," Gordon said, "nobody knows where I am except, of course, Kieran. I hope there's nothing amiss."

He rose and excused himself.

"Do you want me to go with you?" Margaret Anne asked him.

"No, it's okay. You stay put for the moment anyway."

Outside, Gordon picked up the pale, green receiver. To his disbelief it was Zoe's small, nasal voice at the other end of the line.

"Hi, Gordon, what do you think of France? Remember when you promised to take me there?"

"What the hell do you want, and where did you get this number, Zoe?"

"I rang the hotel, of course. Your manager gave it to me. I told him it was urgent."

Damn you, Zoe, Gordon said to himself, remembering the aftermath of the last communication from her.

"That's not a very nice way to greet your ex, especially when she's in big trouble," Zoe continued.

What was coming next?

"What's wrong with you, and what business is it of mine anyway?"

"Oh, it's your business all right. Nick has found out that Jason is your son, and he is furious like a wild animal."

This shook Gordon.

"Who told him?"

"Search me. Somebody sent an anonymous letter. Of course I denied it and swore it wasn't true."

"So, what do you want me to do?"

"He'll probably confront you when he meets you in Cannes. I want our stories to jibe."

"Okay. Should I call you after I talk to him at Cannes?"

"Oh, there's no need for that. I'll be there. So will Jason. Wouldn't miss all the fun for the world."

"All right, goodbye," Gordon said drily, his heart thumping.

"Oh, Gordon," she said, before he'd hung up.

"What?"

"Don't worry about this affecting your wife's career. Nick is a true professional in matters like that. When he meets her about the film you can be sure he won't say a word. Bye bye."

Gordon didn't see any point in telling Zoe that Margaret Anne already knew. He held the phone until the receiver buzzed in his ear. Perhaps he shouldn't tell Margaret Anne of this latest development, though. She was so looking forward to the festival, to her chance at stardom. Perhaps he could handle the matter privately and let her enjoy her big moment.

When he returned to the dining room all eyes were upon him.

"Everything okay?" Margaret Anne asked.

"No problems," Gordon lied, "just a small matter that Kieran wanted to discuss with me."

"Why didn't you call me?" Rose asked, disappointed.

"Sorry, Rose. It never occurred to me."

Margaret Anne sensed he was worried as they lay in bed later that night.

"I know you're uptight," she said. "I knew it the moment you came back into the dining room. Come on, Gordon, what's the problem?"

She looked at him so lovingly, so trustingly. It was the same look he often saw in little Kim's eyes.

"Please tell me, Gordon."

He remembered the consequences of the last secret he kept from her. Drawing in his breath, he told her the details of the phone call.

Margaret Anne was genuinely shocked.

"Oh, Gordon, don't worry. I'm sure everything will work out in the end."

"I hope so."

Margaret Anne held him in her arms for a long while.

"I wonder how Nick got to know."

"I haven't a clue, but it's very hard to keep a secret in this world."

CHAPTER 28

Cannes glittered. It was all colour, light, movement, and noise from the moment the cab drove down the Croissette, the main street that wound its way along by the Mediterranean, lined with glorious palm trees. Gordon and Margaret Anne were immediately caught up in the spell of the festival. Cannes was actually pulsating, full of excitement and tumult, with artists sketching and rock singers blaring away. Turning into the Rue d'Antibes, which ran parallel to Croisette, they encountered movement all around them. Wherever they looked they saw perpetual motion, thousands of people flocking in and out of fancy shops and bistros, reporters and camera men all trying to snatch interviews with anybody at all who resembled a film star.

"God, I've never seen such excitement and atmosphere, so many people crammed into one place. They seem to be here from all over the world," Margaret Anne whispered, aglow.

"You bet they are," Gordon replied, fascinated by it all. "You know the Cannes festival is one of the biggest annual media events in the world. They reckon it brings more than three hundred million francs to the city. And this isn't a major city."

"Ici L'Hotel Majestueux," the young cab driver announced as the car came to a halt outside a large building. They paid him, tipping him generously, and alighted. As they entered the foyer the scene that confronted them was chaotic -- hundreds of people babbling in different languages, actors, actresses, some famous, others virtually unknown, TV cameras and media hustling for scoops. They squeezed their way through the crowd to Reception. Nick Benson had booked a room for them, and they checked in. As they were about to call the lift, an American reporter caught sight of Margaret Anne and dashed frantically towards her.

"Mags O'Dowd, the famous jock from San Diego. Where have you been hiding, Mags? What are you up to now?" he asked at the top of his voice, clicking away with his camera all the while. Gordon took her by the arm and tried to lead her away but the reporter hung on like a leech.

"Just a few more questions," he pleaded, "and a few more nice poses. Come on, Mags, be a sport."

"We're tired," Gordon protested, "we've just arrived, another time."

"No time like the present," the little man persisted. "Besides it will be good for her image. So, what are you doing in Cannes, Mags?"

"You guys don't give up, do you?" Gordon remarked, shaking his head as Margaret Anne answered him.

"I star in one of the films."

The little man's appetite was whetted now.

"Wow, you've come a long way. This is some scoop," he said, pushing his tape recorder closer to her.

"Which film is that, is it in competition?"

"Fresh Pastures and no, it's not competing. It's on the market."

"Interesting title, what part do you play?"

"I play Kerry, an Irish cailin."

"So the film was shot in Ireland then?"

"Half of it only, the other half was shot in the States."

"What's the storyline?"

Gordon protested now more strongly and whisked Margaret Anne into the lift.

"It's damn near impossible to get rid of those guys."

Upstairs, the room was luxurious, with two large windows overlooking the street. They had a first class view of the Palais Theatre, where most of the films were shown, directly opposite them.

"This is super," Margaret Anne said as she took the bottle of champagne from the ice bucket on the table beside the window and popped it open.

"To fame and success," Gordon said as their glasses clinked.

They kissed again and again. He took her in his arms and lifted her gently onto the bed. She held him to her as he pushed his hands under her body and lifted her to him. They cleaved together, were joined, became one. As they lay there perfectly fulfilled, there was a gentle tap on the door.

"Who could that be?" she murmured and Gordon pulled on his trousers and answered the door. A young porter stood outside carrying a huge basket of red roses.

"For Mags O'Dowd, sir," he said in heavily accented English.

"Thank you, son," Gordon said, giving him ten francs.

Margaret Anne sat up in bed, excited.

"An admirer already."

Gordon's tone was slightly strained, she noticed. She opened the envelope containing the little card and read from Nick, welcome to Cannes, see me in suite number ten at eleven a.m. tomorrow.

"He didn't waste much time," Gordon remarked.

"Oh Nick is all business and efficiency. I expect he's anxious to make a large profit on the sale of the film. Remember he's had it on the shelf since November or December. Think of what the interest on fifteen million dollars would be."

"I guess you're right. It's a risky business, this film-making. If he tries to bring up Jason though, you tell him to talk to me."

"Oh, don't worry about that. He doesn't know I know after all. And with him it's always business first."

Early the next morning they were awakened by the buzzing of the telephone. Gordon picked it up and Margaret Anne heard him utter five words, "Be there in fifteen minutes," before he banged down the receiver.

"No need to ask who that was," she commented with a wry smile.

"You're dead right, Zoe. She sounds frantic. Nick is giving her a very bad time about Jason. She's threatening all kinds of things. I better go down and see her."

"I'll come with you. Women understand each other a lot better than men do."

The lobby was thronged with bustling people in an air of excitement and glamour which made everyone's heart beat rapidly. Margaret Anne and Gordon slowly made their way through the crowd, looking in all directions for Zoe. They were about to give up the search when the voice sounded over the intercom in accented English.

"Mr Gordon Edwards to the terrace please."

It was almost as crowded out there but a great deal more airy. Zoe had found a table overlooking the sea and the mountains which flanked it. Jason sat beside her drinking a glass of iced coke. Gordon's eyes were instantly rivetted on his blonde, cherubic little son. Margaret Anne eyed Gordon's ex-lover and, at first glance, she had to admit that Zoe was a very attractive woman --tall and slender, her jet-black hair tightly cut, her large violet eyes shimmering. They seemed to betray her every thought and emotion.

"Aren't you going to introduce us?" Margaret Anne asked Gordon after an awkward silence.

"Oh sure, Mags this is Zoe. Zoe, Mags."

"I'm delighted to meet you, Mags. And this is Jason, my son."

As she spoke she looked curiously at Gordon. The little boy was pale and frightened-looking, and it was obvious that he was disturbed. Zoe poured them coffee and, as she did so, Margaret Anne noticed that her hand shook.

"Well, what's the story?" Gordon finally asked her.

Zoe's eyes flashed like bolts of lightning.

"I'm through with that son of a bitch, Benson. In fact, I'm through period."

She was about to launch into a vicious verbal attack when Margaret Anne interrupted.

"Zoe, do you mind if I take Jason for a walk? It will give you two a little privacy."

Zoe nodded and Gordon looked at his watch.

"I'll see you in the room before eleven," he said, grateful that the boy was removed from this scene.

"What are you going to do?" he asked Zoe when they were alone.

"I'm getting out of here and as far away from that pig as I can."

"And he thinks the child is mine?"

"He knows it. And he's made it clear that he won't rear another man's son. Oh Gordon, he's giving me hell."

"Doesn't he love Jason?"

"Love? He doesn't know the meaning of the word. Money and power are his loves. He's never home anyway. The child hardly knows him. And when he does see him he's scared to death of him."

Gordon was crestfallen. What a disaster. His heart was deeply troubled.

"Where will you go?" he asked.

"Back to New York to my parents, for a while anyway. I'll get myself a job, and, who knows, maybe I'll meet someone else."

Gordon sat with his elbows on the table, rubbing his chin with his thumb and index finger. He was thinking strange, confused thoughts, and nothing made sense to him. Finally he asked the question foremost in his mind.

"Where does Jason fit into this picture?"

Zoe laughed, a tense, nervous kind of laugh.

"He doesn't."

Just what he had feared. Gordon was horrified.

"And what's to become of him?"

"Your guess is as good as mine. He's your son too, remember."

She lit a cigarette and sucked on it viciously.

My God, what a heartless bitch, Gordon thought.

"Don't you care about him either?" he asked, almost in tears now.

She didn't reply at once, but eventually she asked him, "Do you want an honest answer?"

"Yes, of course."

"The truth is no, not really. You know me, Gordon. I never was soft on kids. And now I know for sure that they're more hassle than they're worth. Besides, he's cramping my style and ruining my life."

Gordon was speechless. He could feel the colour drain from his face and his sentiments flowed from anger to sadness to sheer fright.

"There's no more to be said for the moment, I guess," he said, his voice dry. He rose from the table.

"I need to talk this over with my wife. Can you stick around Cannes for a while?"

"Don't worry, I'm not going anywhere fast," she said, stubbing out her cigarette.

"I'll pick Jason up in your room later."

CHAPTER 29

When Margaret Anne saw Gordon coming through the bedroom door, she could guess what had transpired. It was quite obvious that he was deeply troubled.

Entering in a distracted state, Gordon suddenly focused across the room on his son. Jason sat there contentedly watching television and munching all sorts of goodies. From the way Gordon stared at him the boy might have been doing something miraculous.

"Well, how did it go?" Margaret Anne asked him.

"We have to talk, Mags," he said, tearing his eyes away from Jason and looking pleadingly at her.

"Yes, of course, love," she replied tenderly.

"But it's past eleven and I have this meeting with Nick. Will it hold until afterwards?"

"Sure," he replied, meekly kissing her.

"But remember what I said, and watch that guy," he warned as she went through the door.

Alone with his son, he felt awkward and disoriented. The little fellow didn't even seem to notice his presence. Gordon walked to the window and stood there with his hands dug deeply in his pockets. Thousands of people stood outside the Palais, trying to get a glimpse of the film stars. Through the window he saw the Gendarme lining the steps, and behind them the media struggling for strategic positions. Clint Eastwood was starring in this morning's film, so it was a huge attraction.

The sight of all the glamour and splendour made Gordon suddenly realise where he really was, and why he'd really come here -- to see his wife's launch into international stardom. Poor Mags, he thought. One of the biggest highlights of her life ruined by a huge problem from my past. There's always something, he thought bitterly.

Meanwhile, in Nick Benson's suite, the meeting was in full swing. Matters were proceeding very pleasantly and Margaret Anne was relieved that she could sit there in his presence without being too disturbed. There was still that fire and energy behind his eyes, but now they did not captivate her. She'd been a little nervous going in, as it was her first meeting with him since the shooting of the film. As he sat there at the top of the long table in the huge lounge, a fat cigar in his mouth, she wondered what she'd ever really seen in him at all.

Guy Petrassi sat on his right, swallowing champagne as if it were water. Across from him sat three other board members of the film company. The cast of the film, most of whom Margaret Anne had met, were also present.

Two exceptions, however, were Gabrielle Freeman and John Stern, who had not been involved in the Irish shoot. Gabrielle was very beautiful, of medium height, her glossy hair almost luminous, and her mouth full and sensuous. But what came forth from this full, sensuous mouth was a loud, almost raucous voice which grated heavily on one's nerves. John was equally attractive, but in a masculine way. He was sallow-skinned, brown-eyed, and had a lovely, sensitive face.

Margaret Anne stopped looking around as Nick called for everyone's attention.

"We are very lucky," he began, "that Giles Jacob chose our film to be shown here. It's a great honour and privilege, and a good omen also. Giles Jacob is renowned for sniffing out the good ones, and ours is one of just five to be shown out of competition. If the jury like it we're all made, we'll have lots of offers, and we'll come out with a handsome profit. And you can't imagine what it will do for all your careers. It'll be screened in the Palais a week from today. It's an evening performance and it's formal dress, kids."

On and on he went for long minutes, during which Margaret Anne's thoughts constantly flashed back to Gordon.

Guy Petrassi then gave them detailed information on press conferences and radio and television interviews. He showed them the reams of promotional material that would be plastered all over the town. They were definitely doing an excellent marketing job. At the end of the two hour meeting they each received a glossy package giving them all the relevant information.

"Come for some lunch, Mags?" Nick asked her casually afterwards.

"No thanks."

Nick did not hide his disappointment.

"What's with you?" he asked her. She didn't know about the kid, did she? he wondered.

"I've got things to do, and, besides, I'm not hungry."

"Well here's something that should perk up your appetite. I've got the lead part for you in our next film. Interested?"

Nick smiled when Margaret Anne's jaw dropped. He loved having that power over people. Had the whole Jason business influenced him to make this offer? he asked himself Damn right, it had. He knew making this film would take her away from Gordon for months. And he knew once he and Margaret Anne were working intensely together the unmistakable attraction between them would once again flare up. And this time he'd be sure to act on it. But then again, he decided, he'd never offer her the part just to get at Gordon. It was undeniable that she was good, very good, she belonged up on the screen. If he could manage both to hurt that bastard and get her on screen with one move, then of course he'd offer her the part.

"I'll have to think about it. I'll get back to you," she said.

Nick Benson almost swallowed his cigar

"Am I hearing right? Say that again."

"I said I'll have to think about it."

"Think about it? Are you out of your mind, Mags?" he yelled. "This is what you want. Your big break."

"I know it is. I'll let you know as soon as I can," she replied, leaving the suite.

Nick was wide-eyed and open-mouthed. If that's not looking a gift horse in the mouth. And all the talented actors and actresses who'd kill for an offer like he'd just made.

CHAPTER 30

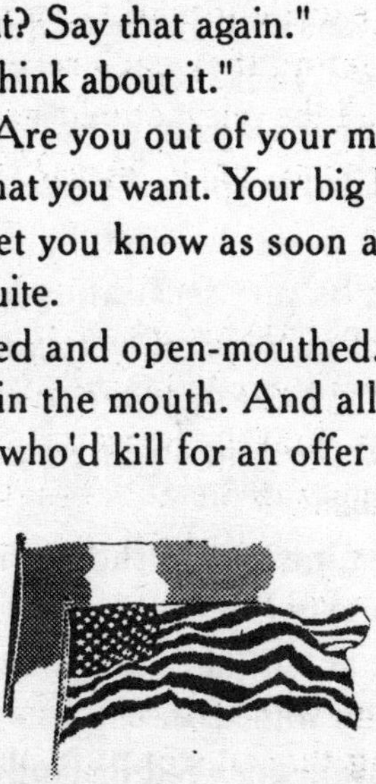

Gordon was seated in an armchair by the window when Margaret Anne came through the door. She looked around the room.

"Where's Jason?" she asked.

"Zoe came and collected him a little while ago."

"How did you get along with him?"

"Not much communication really. I watched a kids movie with him. He liked it a lot and I enjoyed it too, you know, just being with him."

"That was nice." She kicked off her shoes and looked out the window as well.

"Enjoying the side show, I see," she said.

"You bet, the excitement out there is something else. I saw Linda Evans and Stephen Spielberg and --"

"Oh, there's Tom Cruise!" she interrupted with a shriek, almost jumping out of her skin.

Gordon smiled in spite of himself.

"It's strange to see them off the screen, in the flesh as it were. It must be very frustrating for them -- no privacy, no freedom of movement, constantly mobbed by media and fans. No wonder there are so many suicides."

"Still there's nothing like being a star. Who wouldn't jump at the chance?"

"Which reminds me, I should have asked you. How did the meeting go?"

"We'll talk about that later. First I'm anxious to hear how you got on with Zoe."

His expression changed instantly and he cast his eyes downwards.

Her heart went out to him.

"Let's go out for lunch," she suggested softly, "and we can talk then. Maybe a little drink or two would loosen your tongue."

They lunched at La Mère Besson, one of the best restaurants in Cannes, and after a few glasses of cool, white wine, Gordon began to relax.

"Would you like to talk about it now?" Margaret Anne asked him as she held his hand across the table.

"It's some dilemma, Mags. You'll never believe it."

"Try me," she replied with a curious kind of smile.

Gordon polished off the remainder of his wine.

"The bottom line is Nick has no time at all for the boy. He knows damn well he's my son. And his mother doesn't want him either. He's more hassle than he's worth and he's cramping her style. That's what her son means to her."

He looked Margaret Anne straight in the eyes, trying to gauge her reaction. He didn't see any surprise registered there, which amazed him.

"I knew all that already," she announced quite casually.

"You knew? How?"

"Oh, I know, believe me. I know just where Zoe's coming from. How can I even criticise her? I felt exactly the same way about my own son. She's just like I was. Life sure has some strange quirks of fate. Or, as Mum would say, God's ways are wonderful."

Gordon noticed a strange, distant look in her eyes.

"I hope this isn't upsetting you too much, love," he said tenderly.

"Not at all," she replied. "I've come to terms with that long ago. I'm at peace with myself now and I'll never look back. Anyway, Bikram is far better off with his own people. But what about Jason?"

"I don't know."

"Well, what do you think? Do you love the boy?"

Gordon hesitated.

"Well," he said at last, "I don't really know him. But the moment I laid eyes on him I felt the strongest urge to take him in my arms and protect him."

Near tears, Margaret Anne whispered, "That's only natural. Blood really is thicker than water, I guess."

There was a long silence then. Margaret Anne thought very hard. One part of her desperately longed to act again. She'd never known such fulfilment as she had during those months. But she also saw only one solution to Gordon's dilemma. Could she do both? She was young and strong. If she turned this opportunity down she'd never get another. The film would only take a matter of months, after all, and then she'd be back at home with her family. Why couldn't she do both? She'd make Gordon happy and herself happy. She decided to take care of Gordon's end first.

"Let's bring Jason home to live with us," she said. "I know that would make you very happy."

Gordon was totally overcome.

"Oh Mags, do you mean it?"

"Of course I mean it. I think he's a darling, and he'll be great company for Kim."

He kissed her across the table.

"I love you, Mags O'Dowd-Edwards. You'll never know what this means to me."

"We'd better get a lawyer to draw up some kind of sound legal agreement, that's vital, you know. We don't want Zoe playing chess with us whenever the humour strikes her. I know, I did it myself."

"I guess you're right. I'll get on to that right away."

"And Gordon, speaking of playing chess with people, there's something I'd like to do."

"What's that?"

"Have Gavin be Jason's godfather. I know I can never make up for what I did to him, but at least it's a gesture. It's time we made our peace, don't you think?"

Gordon pictured Gavin giving little Jason rides in his wheelchair and smiled.

"I think that's a great idea."

CHAPTER 31

During the remainder of the week, the crowds in the street and the sense of excitement grew. Margaret Anne found herself caught up in a crazy merry-go-round of press releases, radio and television interviews, parties that went on into the early hours, and a multitude of photographs that almost made her snap. A few days before the Fresh Pastures premiere, Gordon Edwards saw to it that her picture was everywhere, and then, bingo, she was known. She was a celebrity, a star again, just like that, and the crowds flocked around her, men, women, and children, brandishing pens and papers for autographs.

"This is crazy," she remarked to Gordon. "They're like sheep led on by this media hype. They don't care about the quality of the film or the acting. They're just totally caught up in this fantasy world. It's mass hysteria, that's what I call it."

Gordon was terrific, so calming and supportive through it all. She would have cracked up several times if he wasn't at her side. It was all so bizarre.

The day they went shopping for her evening dress for the premiere was one she would never forget. The morning was dull, hot, and humid so she decided to dress in a pair of tattered, denim shorts, a blue, sleeveless t-shirt, and large, dark sunglasses.

"Would you know me in the street, if you saw me?" she asked Gordon as she looked at herself from all angles in the full length mirror.

"Let me see now," he said, scrutinising her closely, chuckling under his breath. God, he would know her a mile off. But maybe others might not. After some deliberation he replied, "No, definitely not. In fact, I'd pass you on the street."

"Great," she exclaimed triumphantly.

"Let's go. I hope this get-up works."

They walked the streets for several hours, in and out of crowded boutiques, virtually unnoticed. Her disguise was working, and, despite her exhaustion and frustration, for that she was grateful. As they climbed the elevator to the fashion department of Florentine's, Gordon tapped her on the shoulder.

"This is our last shot," he warned. "Let's hope we get something nice here."

"God, we'd better," Margaret Anne said, close to panic.

Thankfully they had quite a nice selection of evening wear. After several minutes of frantic searching, finally their choice was narrowed down to two gowns. The white one, however, didn't seem to fall properly. It definitely looked nicer in the hand.

"This must be the one, then," Gordon said, offering her the magnificent, full-length, kelly-green dress. Margaret Anne retired to the dressing room while he hoped and prayed they had at last hit the jackpot. Suddenly Gordon heard a loud, panicked scream from her dressing room. He jumped into action.

"My God," he exclaimed, fear gripping him as he ran to her. He was just in time to catch the small, olive-skinned photographer as he scurried out of the dressing room. Gordon was furious, this was the last straw. He caught the photographer by the collar, pinned him to the wall with one hand, and grabbed his camera with the other. He let loose of the collar and the photographer collapsed on the ground as Gordon opened the camera and exposed the film.

"Get the hell out of here, you sleazy little wimp," he roared. The man lifted himself up and scurried away while Gordon went to his wife.

She was standing there motionless in her bra and panties, the big tears rolling down her flushed cheeks.

"Oh Gordon," she cried, falling into his arms.

"It was awful. I got such a shock."

"It's okay now, take it easy. I've got the film right here."

On the evening of the premiere Gordon realised he had never seen Margaret Anne look so ravishing. She seemed to be sculpted into the exquisite, kelly-green, silk gown. It hung gracefully off her shoulders, displaying three strands of glistening pearls, and her hair was swept up in a matching kelly-green bow.

Although the Palais was right across the road, tradition demanded that they be taken by festival car, driven right around the theatre, and back again to the front entrance.

As the cast of the film and their partners got out of the cars, the thousands of fans began to cheer. Margaret Anne was carried away by the thrill and exhilaration of it all and she began to wave expansively. She took Gordon's arm with her free hand and thought how handsome ...oked in his white tuxedo and dark, wine bow tie. And at least one American fan seemed to share her view.

"Isn't he cute?" Margaret Anne overheard as they passed and moved along up the wide staircase with the plush, red carpet. The pomp and splendour were enhanced by the strains of a band playing processional music from within.

Inside, as the lights went down, Margaret Anne was charged with anticipation. She didn't quite know what to expect, seeing the movie for the first time. It was a strange experience, seeing oneself on screen. Highly emotional, she felt the goose pimples rise. As the movie progressed she was spellbound. It was brilliant; she could hardly believe her eyes. Everything looked so much more beautiful than her recollection of the shooting would have suggested. It came alive before her eyes and there was a warmth and atmosphere that totally captivated her. What a difference editing and background music makes, she thought. They sure can make a silk purse out of a sow's ear. Wouldn't it be wonderful to enter that magic world again?

"What do you think of it?" she whispered to Gordon.

"It's fantastic, super, absolutely fabulous. And a wonderful piece of acting by my wife. I'm proud of you," he said, squeezing her hand tightly.

Before she knew it, it was over. The credits rolled, the lights went up, and there was thunderous applause as the spot lights hit the cast. It was a wonderful moment. The movie had gone down well, of that there was no doubt.

Nick was in high spirits later in the nightclub upstairs.

"We're in business, we've done it! All the right people were here. I love you all!"

He danced around the floor in sheer delight. Spotting Margaret Anne and Gordon sitting quietly at a small table in an alcove, he bounded over to them. He leaned forward and unashamedly embraced Margaret Anne.

"You were divine," he said and smiled, keeping his back to Gordon all the while.

"Come dance with me."

A wave of fury mounted inside Gordon as he watched, but he decided not to spoil the evening for Margaret Anne. This, after all, is what she wanted.

Nick took her by the hand and led her out onto the floor.

"How about that offer I made you?" he asked. "I bet you've decided after tonight."

She had decided. She'd been thinking intensely, ever since the euphoria she'd felt as the credits rolled. Looking out at the sea of applauding hands and smiling faces it had struck her very clearly that she could not be a star without sacrificing everything else. It was the price one had to pay. Nick twirled her dizzily around the dance floor and when the song neared its end, she whispered her decision in his ear.

The music stopped. Nick speechlessly watched her return to Gordon. A few moments later he saw them leave, arm in arm.

CHAPTER 32

The following morning they slept late. It was the sound of the telephone ringing that eventually roused them. It was Zoe.

"Did you hear the news?"

Her shrill voice grated on Gordon's ears.

"What news?"

"The movie got rave reviews. Nick has made a fabulous deal with a huge Australian film company."

"Good for him," Gordon replied in a less than enthusiastic tone.

"By the way," she continued, "I've signed that legal thingy. When are you leaving?"

"Tomorrow, very early in the morning."

"I'll drop Jason off tonight then, okay?"

"That'll be fine," he said and replaced the receiver abruptly.

"Will I ever see the back of that woman?" he muttered half under his breath.

Margaret Anne ran her fingers through his hair.

"Don't be so hard on her. It's not like you. Just think of the favour she did for you. Aren't you glad to be getting your son?"

"You bet I am," he assured her.

"I could never be happy thinking about Nick Benson raising him."

"And you'll be happy spending lots of time with Jason?"

"Yes, very happy."

"Listen to me, Gordon. Last night I made a very important decision, a decision which is going to have a huge impact on you, on Kim, and on Jason."

"Yes, what was this decision?" Gordon asked nervously.

"I'll tell you when we get to Rose's and the whole family is together, all right? I don't want you to think it was just the glamour and excitement of this place that made me decide."

"Mags --"

"Promise me you'll let me tell you in my own time. Tomorrow."

"It won't be easy, but all right. I suppose I can wait one day. So then, what would you like to do today?"

"Not a thing," she replied emphatically.

"Let's have a lazy, relaxing day, just you and I."

"That's the best idea I've heard for a long time," Gordon said, reaching for the phone to order breakfast from room service.

"This is the life," Margaret Anne remarked, sitting up in bed munching a delicious croissant which oozed with strawberry jam.

They spent the remainder of the day in the security and comfort of the luxurious room, with the curtains drawn to block out the world outside. They drank coffee, read the newspapers, made love, drank more coffee, watched television, and made love again. Later in the evening, showered and dressed, they dined in the room on caviar and champagne.

Gordon lifted his long, fluted glass to hers "Here's to Mags O'Dowd, the most radiant, beautiful star in the world."

"And here's to Gordon Edwards, manager par excellence."

They were slightly tipsy when Zoe arrived to hand Jason over. The boy was dressed in pyjamas, dressing gown, and slippers, ready for bed, and he fell into Margaret Anne's arms. Zoe was flabbergasted and Gordon was immensely relieved. He'd been dreading this moment of separation.

"Will you join us for a drink?" Gordon asked her.

"I'd love to, but Nick is waiting for me. We're going to a party on Guy's yacht. Have to run, you know how impatient he is."

"You and Nick are back together?"

"Oh, yes. We've fallen in love again."

Gordon shook his head.

"I guess in the end you're very grateful to whoever sent Nick that anonymous letter then."

"Yes, I thank myself every day. I knew all along it was that brat who was driving us apart."

Gordon was shocked, watching her step across the room to kiss their son goodbye. There was no sign of emotion on either side of the kiss.

"Goodbye Jason, remember what I told you, be a good boy."

"Okay, Mom," he replied and she was gone. That was it, as easy as that. Margaret Anne made a comfortable bed for Jason on the couch, Gordon told him a story, and in no time he was fast asleep.

But as they drove towards Avignon the next morning, Jason was aglow with excitement.

"I can't wait to see Ireland. Mom says it's like Fairyland."

"I know you'll love it. But first we must collect your new baby sister," Margaret Anne told him.

"Gosh, I'm glad I have a sister. I've always wanted a sister."

"And I bet she'll be glad to have a big brother like you to take care of her."

Kim was on the terrace with Rose when they arrived, looking more beautiful than ever and as brown as a berry. She hadn't forgotten her parents at all. They were relieved as she waved her hands and kicked her legs with excitement.

"You've taken great care of her, thanks a million," Margaret Anne said, but Rose did not hear. She was staring at the boy.

"This is Jason, my son," Gordon introduced the child.

Rose was speechless for a second or two.

"He's your son all right," she finally said.

"My God, he is the very image of you."

Margaret Anne called her aside and whispered, "We'll explain later."

"And congratulations on your wonderful success," Rose said.

"We read all about you in the papers. It must have been the experience of a lifetime."

"It had its moments," Margaret Anne replied.

Later at dinner they told Rose and Jean the story of Jason. There were tears in her eyes as she addressed Gordon.

"Imagine going to Cannes to see the premiere of your wife's film and returning with your son. It's just wonderful, like something you'd read about in a book. You have a boy and a girl now. Some people have all the luck," she remarked wistfully.

"Don't give up hope," Gordon told her jovially. "Remember the old saying."

"Which one is that?"

"If at first you don't succeed, try try again."

Jean was highly amused.

"Très bien, très bien and very true also," he winked at Rose.

As Gordon and Mags lay in bed that night, enfolded in each others arms, they talked well into the night. They went back over the events of the past two weeks, made plans for the future of the hotel, and wondered how Jason would settle down with them.

"It's time I told you my decision," Mags said eventually.

Gordon shifted nervously in the darkness.

"I'd been wondering when you would."

"I didn't tell you," Margaret Anne started, "that Nick Benson offered me the lead in his next film."

Gordon felt something give way in his heart. But this is what she's always wanted, he thought. There was no stopping her from becoming a star.

"Congratulations," he managed to say.

"I turned it down," she whispered, watching her husband's eyes light up. He held her closer and kissed her.

"Oh Mags, I'm so glad. But curious also. Why?"

"Because I was offered a far nicer part from someone else."

His face fell again.

"You mean you got a second offer?"

"Yes, I did."

"From who, the Australian Company?"

"No," she said, her eyes holding a strange, mysterious look. "I was asked by the most handsome, talented director in the world to play the beautiful role of wife and mother."

He was puzzled when she began to speak, but then the penny dropped, and his eyes filled with tears of joy.

"Mags, I love you. Those are the most wonderful words I've ever heard. They'll remain forever engraved on my heart."

EPILOGUE

The sun behind the hills of Kilbawn was setting like a big, red ball of fire. Below them the sea shimmered. Yachts and boats bobbed gently up and down in the harbour. It was one of those balmy nights when the countryside was radiantly green and fragrant with the sweet scents of flowers in bloom and new-mown hay.

Margaret Anne and Gordon sat together out on the patio in front of the sun lounge. They'd been silent for a while, perfectly silent, each of them lost in thought, enjoying being together, out where it was so peaceful.

Gordon closed his eyes and relaxed, letting the tensions of a very busy day at the hotel ebb away from him.

Again he experienced the rush of happiness and excitement as he thought of his loving wife beside him and his son and daughter fast asleep in bed. He looked at the toys scattered on the lawn in front of him. Jason had settled down like a dream and he and Kim were the greatest of playmates. It seemed as though Jason had always been with them, and he couldn't imagine life without him now.

Margaret Anne sighed. She could still see Sean the postman, lean and fit with his weatherbeaten complexion, as he handed her the letter. That was just a week ago. The news had saddened her and even now she felt the tears welling up again in her eyes. Father Dom had been found dead in his cell, with a letter to her on the table beside his bed, ready to be posted. One of his superiors sent her a short note informing her along with his letter.

She remembered the words he'd written, and she could see him standing there, and hear his voice as he spoke them to her. He was so grateful for the holiday in Ireland, so glad to see Gordon and herself so happy and blessed. What a pity he hadn't seen their son. But of course he sees him now. Isn't he in heaven looking down at him? Thank you so much Dom, her heart said, thank you for showing me the real meaning of life.

"Don't thank me, thank the Good Lord who loves you, and who sought you out," she heard him say again, as he had so often in the past.

Despite this loss, the telephone call from France had gladdened her. Rose had just been informed by the doctor that she was pregnant, and she was walking on air. Her happiness would soon be complete. Funny how life goes, people come into the world and other people leave it. Her father had always said that it was just as natural to die as it was to be born. She felt Gordon's strong arms around her, and he held her close to him.

"Isn't it great to be home? There's no place like it."

She looked lovingly into his eyes and smiled. "I couldn't agree more. I'm so happy now, so very happy. And so very much at peace."